About the Author

Rachel Armstrong has always loved making up stories and has never wanted to be anything but an author. She writes contemporary romantic fiction ranging from rural to suspense. Rachel enjoys creating epic feel-good stories and has a weakness for an adventurous holiday escape. Helping her characters find their happily-ever-after is her life's joy.

Rachel lives in Townsville, Queensland, with her border collie, Jacob, where she helps people live their best lives as an exercise physiologist. In her spare time, she is either reading on her treadmill or plotting out her next novel while grooving at Zumba. Rachel's a keen traveller and has enjoyed many holidays exploring historic London, flying through the Grand Canyon, and hiking volcanos in Bali.

Rachel enjoys connecting with readers on social media and through her website.

www.rachelarmstrongauthor.com.au

RACHEL ARMSTRONG

The Pub with No Food

Pink Paws Publishing

First published 2023

ISBN 978-0-6453555-4-3

THE PUB WITH NO FOOD
© 2023 by Rachel Armstrong

The characters in this book are a work of fiction and have no existence outside the imagination of the author and have no relation whatsoever to anyone bearing the same name or names. They are not even distantly inspired by any individual known or unknown to the author, and all incidents are pure invention.

Published by
Pink Paws Publishing
Rachel Armstrong
Townsville QLD 4810
Australia

A catalogue record for this book is available from the National Library of Australia
www.librariesaustralia.nla.gov.au

For Mum and Ian

Thank you for helping make my 2023
Christmas wish come true.

Dear Reader,

Merry Christmas from Elizadale! It is bright and sunny, sweltering hot, and sometimes even pouring down rain during December in North Queensland, but nothing deters the holiday spirit. So thank you for choosing to read Grace and Luke's story, whatever time of the year it is, in the first spin-off Elizadale novella, a prequel to the Shadow Creek series.

This story was written well after I'd completed the series as part of a group effort to produce Christmas novellas. Uninspired, I decided to tell Grace and Luke's story while throwing in everything I loved about the holiday season. It was spicy, fun, but lacked depth. Thankfully, when I reinvented Elizadale, Grace and Luke both received a new role in the community. She has brought yoga to town and Luke has launched a new menu at his family's pub. I was very excited to rewrite this one and weave in their new storylines, so I hope you enjoy it as much as I do.

Christmas isn't a pleasant time for Grace, which I'm sure people from dysfunctional families can relate to. All she wants is to enjoy the holiday as much as her friends, with peace, quiet, and love. Perhaps by falling for her best friend's brother, she might finally find the family she's been looking for.

I wish you all good tidings and hope you enjoy the merriment of a warm, Aussie Christmas.

Happy reading,

Rachel

Chapter One

Grace White drew in a deep breath as she paced the homestead kitchen. Her fists clenched and she exhaled slowly, focusing on her pranayama technique to calm her nerves.

It didn't work.

'Matt Clark might be wealthy and handsome, Dad. But I'm not going to marry him.'

Her father crossed his thick arms over his barrel chest and glared at her. His reaction wasn't unexpected. Edward had never cared about what she wanted and why she still longed for his respect she didn't know.

'Why not?'

Grace rolled her eyes. Why? Because they weren't dating? She didn't love him? Matt had never asked? Because it was the twenty-first century when arranged marriages were a thing of the past and she lived in a country where, as a daughter, she wasn't a commodity to trade?

Her father could take his pick.

'Because I have no interest in being used as a pawn in your manipulative schemes,' she said instead. 'Do you even know Matt? Do you know if he's the kind of man I'd want to be with? No. All you see are the acres he's set to inherit, his family's Brahman stud, and the profit you can make out of it all!'

Not to mention the last thing Grace would do was marry a cattleman. She had escaped the cattle station she'd grown up on—the dirt, the isolation, the smell—and she didn't want to live on another one. She belonged in town where she had friends and her job as a nurse at the local medical centre.

'I want what's best for you, Grace!' Edward's arms dropped to his sides and her gaze fell to his clenched fists. Her father had never hit her, but Grace wouldn't put it past him.

'No, you don't. You want what's best for yourself. Marrying someone I don't love will never be best for me.'

'But you have no problem screwing him. Fucking hell, girl, you'll give the bloke the wrong idea!'

Grace resisted a wince as the bitter taste of regret rose in her throat. She hated how her father spoke to her. And while it had been fun, her steamy night with Matt Clark at the Mareeba Rodeo was one mistake Grace wished she could take back. Part of her had known better. She'd been attending the rodeo with her friends when the gorgeous man she'd flirted with a few times in Elizadale had approached her in jeans, boots, and a rodeo buckle he sported with pride. Matt wasn't Grace's usual type, but she rarely had any fun and truth was, she'd liked him.

But after an early morning dash back to her room the following day, her father had reintroduced them. Only then had she learned Matt was of the Clark family who owned Redback Station, the property that shared the northern border with their own. White Peaks was small in comparison and on the outskirts of their township of Elizadale, so Grace's family had rarely interacted with those on Redback. Not that the

Clarks lived there. They were cattle barons who lived on the range in Toowoomba and employed people to do the hard work. Matt had all the charm of a rich landowner and packed quite a punch in the looks department too, with a grin designed to weaken a woman's knees. She'd been a fool and fallen for it. And ended up in his bed.

After the events that night, when Matt had scored the best time in the bareback bronc ride, he'd had another woman hanging off his arm and Grace had realised the true depth of her stupidity. Matt Clark was a known playboy with no intentions of giving any woman a second date, let alone settling down. She might not have invested her heart in their fling, but it had still hurt.

Her father seemed to have other ideas though and while Matt had been back and forth from town this past year, he would soon move to Redback to take over as manager. The invitation to spend Christmas with him had come out of the blue, but since her father had known about it, Grace smelled manipulation. And found great satisfaction in telling him she wasn't going.

She had plans for the upcoming year and they didn't involve Matt Clark or marriage.

'What I do, Dad, is my business. And apart from that, you can't "sell" me off for your own personal gain like you did Aunt Cynthia. You want me to marry for land? To gain you more contacts in the cattle industry? Well, too bad. I don't want to live on a farm, especially a cattle one.'

'Here we go,' he grumbled, his eyes flaring. 'The fluffy animal debate again.'

Grace clenched her teeth. 'It's not a fluffy animal debate! There are current guidelines to cattle farming that are less cru …' She trailed off. There were some things she'd rile her father up about, but others she knew to steer clear of. 'You could treat the cows better,' she muttered.

'It's what's done, Grace. We raise them, fatten them up, then send them to slaughter so that we can eat!'

'But there are better ways … you don't have to …' Grace shook her head. She couldn't have this argument again. She'd tried telling her father that his farming methods were old-school and barbaric, but Edward refused to listen.

Instead, Grace addressed the other subject. 'Look, I'm not going to Toowoomba for Christmas and that's final. I'm not interested in Matt, nor am I interested in marriage right now.'

'You're twenty-four years old!'

'Exactly! I should be working and travelling and making my dreams come true!'

Edward scoffed. 'What dreams?'

Grace crossed her arms. Like she hadn't already told him. 'I'm opening a yoga studio.'

If her father rolled his eyes one more time, they'd fall out of his thick head. 'What crap. No one around here wants to do fucking yoga.'

'Yes, they do! The studio is popular in Mareeba, but it's forty minutes away, and people I've spoken to are keen to try it.'

'Maybe for a week before they realise it's bullshit.'

Grace's shoulders sagged. No matter how much she was used to it, his derision still hurt.

The back door opened and Francesca White strolled into the kitchen. Grace's heart sank further. Her mother wouldn't take her side on the marriage or the yoga issue. Francesca would never understand Grace's desire to live and work in town when she'd been an acre-chaser herself.

'What's all this yelling?'

Edward exhaled and crossed his arms over his protruding belly. 'The vegan hippy has ended things with Matt Clark.'

'I'm not a hippy! Or vegan! And I was never *with* Matt!'

Her mother's disappointed eyes landed on her. 'Oh, Grace. He was a good choice for you. His family owns many properties.'

Grace stared at her parents. Did they *have* ears? She could see them sticking out the side of their thick heads, so why didn't they use them? Why couldn't they support her dreams like loving parents should?

'He'll set you up for life,' Edward added. 'And the two of you can help your brother.'

'Yeah, because by marrying Matt, you and Charlie can exploit Redback to save White Peaks, isn't that right?' Grace turned on her heel. 'Forget it. I'm out of here.'

She didn't get far before her mother blocked her exit. 'Don't talk to us like that, young lady. We just want what's best for you.'

'No, you don't. You want to use me, but I'm not a commodity to trade.'

Grace left the house, slamming the flyscreen door behind her. She stormed off the aging verandah, down the dusty front path, and slipped into her lime green Mazda 2, blinking back tears.

Why had she thought she could get through to him? Her father was impervious to change.

Taking a deep breath, Grace started the car and drove away from her childhood home. She'd done what she had to do. She didn't know why Matt had invited her for Christmas, but she had every right to decline when she barely knew the man. If Edward wanted to be angry about that, then fine. She would never win. He'd been angry with her since she'd left home after high school to start an admin job at the Mareeba Hospital. She'd been thrilled at such an opportunity, but her father had wanted her in Elizadale. Then Grace had decided to study nursing and he'd ranted and raved about that too. He'd hardly supported her finishing high school, let alone university.

Shoving aside the hurt, Grace turned onto the highway. Her father might not approve, but what did Grace have if not her dreams? She'd loved the years she'd spent studying in Cairns as not only had she enjoyed nursing, but also discovering yoga had changed her life. The strength and flexibility she'd found in her body had boosted her energy and empowered her emotionally. Her confidence had grown and she'd found peace of mind, two things she'd lacked after growing up with her parents. Now Grace wanted to bring that joy to the people in Elizadale.

And she would. Hope filled her heart as she drove south towards the beautiful small town she loved to call home. White Peaks spread into the distance on her right, while the Kellys' coffee farm occupied the thousands of acres on her left. Their two farms, along with Tropic Sun and Shadow Creek, were the four major enterprises in Elizadale, but there were many smaller farms as well with impressive turnover. Produce lay at the heart of their community and part of Grace understood her father's wish for her to marry into a neighbouring property, but he'd almost blown a gasket when she'd started dating Shadow Creek heir, Adam Maguire.

Grace's heart twisted at the memories. She had just returned from university when she'd been drawn to the local bad boy, who, along with his brother, would inherit the sprawling banana farm. Their romance had been easy, fun, and they'd fallen head over heels for each other. But her father hadn't been happy. Edward had threatened Adam, which Adam and his devil-may-care attitude had only found amusing. But while the threats had been empty, they'd still scared her. Edward also had personal issues with local farmers and there'd been arguments at the pub, but Grace had never witnessed those. She had enough trouble being Edward White's daughter without seeing firsthand what he was capable of. Her father was nasty and after six months of dating under Edward's wrath, the spark had diminished between her and Adam and they'd called it quits.

Sometimes, when she was feeling lonely, Grace wished she'd fought harder. Adam was a good man and at least life on a banana farm didn't involve the stench and crying of cattle. But it'd been for the best because while she'd enjoyed their time together, she'd since realised they weren't right for each other.

Perhaps she wasn't right for anyone.

Grace winced. She shouldn't think like that because she enjoyed dating and hoped to marry one day. She just didn't want it to result from her father's manipulation.

All she wanted was stability and happiness, which was why she was opening this studio. She could make a success of it, she was sure.

Chapter Two

'I wouldn't worry, Luke. With Christmas coming up, I'm sure revenue will increase.'

Luke Smithfield studied his sister on the other side of the desk as he leaned back in his chair. He wasn't so sure. With liquor laws and polices getting tighter and the increase in the cost of alcohol, it was becoming harder to sustain a profitable pub. They weren't in financial trouble, but he didn't like the figures and couldn't sit back and be as nonchalant about it as Jessica. Together, they shared a forty per cent interest in the Smithfield Hotel and when their parents had left on their road trip three months ago, Luke had officially taken over as manager. But while his father had always valued his input, this was his chance to prove he could take the pub into the future, and he needed to put his dream to the test.

'Christmas is busy,' he agreed. 'But I think it's long past time we gave the menu a makeover.'

Jessica frowned. 'What's wrong with the menu?'

Luke exhaled between his teeth. What wasn't wrong with it? Steak, schnitzels, chips, and not a carrot in sight, let alone any other vegetable. 'There's nothing worth eating. It's boring and the same as every other pub. So, I was thinking …' He leaned forward. 'Let's make Smithy's the place people in Elizadale come for a *nice* meal. We'll throw out the pub grub and serve some gourmet main dishes. I'm thinking nachos, stir-fry, veggie burgers, salmon …'

A knowing gleam filled his sister's eyes. 'You want to go healthy, don't you?'

Luke shrugged. 'I want variety. Something that's interesting. We should utilise our quiet dining room and have a menu that's worth raving about. I want to throw out the garlic bread and replace it with ciabatta and dips. Maybe add a variety of grilled fish choices and make interesting salads. And yeah, if I can throw out the deep fryers and sell only baked potato, I'll be a happy man.'

He cared about health, fitness, and nutrition, and he wouldn't apologise for it. Besides, everyone liked a good baked potato and steamed veggies were far tastier than a side of limp greens passed off as 'salad'. He couldn't go wrong with lasagne and gourmet burgers. He'd keep the steaks, but why not offer baked salmon and grilled mackerel over the deep-fried version that came wrapped in butchers paper from the takeaway shop?

Jessica laughed. 'You know, that wouldn't be the worst idea since air fryers are all the craze these days.'

'Exactly. So, you're on board?'

'You know I'll always support you. The question is, will Bill?'

Luke paused as he recalled the conversation he'd had with the cook last week. 'He grumbled about it, but I think he'll come around and we can be ready by New Year.'

'Yes, don't go changing anything this close to Christmas. We'll be busy with all the parties we have booked. But things might quieten that week before New Year, so we could have time to pull it off.'

'I think so.' Grinning, Luke stood. 'I guess we should get out there though. The Friday rush is bound to have started.'

Jessica rose to her feet and straightened her Smithfield Hotel singlet over the waistband of her jeans. 'Do you want to serve the bistro bar, or should I?'

'I will.' Luke placed the finance books on the shelf behind his desk. 'You go help Tina and I'll be there in a minute.'

Jessica left and Luke tidied up before heading out to help. At six o'clock on a Friday evening, the pub steadily filled as people mingled at tables and around the bar. Jessica flipped beer caps and laughed with the young men who enjoyed flirting with her. He didn't like it, but Luke had long ago accepted that he couldn't change nature. Men liked pretty girls and Jessica was stunning with her long blonde hair and wicked smile. But she owned her sass, could handle herself, and the locals treated her with respect.

They wouldn't dare not to while Luke was around.

As he crossed the room, regulars waved and sent him cheery hellos from the high tables. One thing Smithy's had going for it was that they were a modern pub compared to the Royal Hotel, which had been the first building completed after Stuart Riley had settled Elizadale some hundred and fifty years ago. He had nothing against the Royal as it was popular, historic, and he respected Georgina Kincade as a businesswoman, but Smithy's defining quality was their quiet bistro with its magnificent glass-fronted entrance. The bar and fridges separated the two rooms, allowing service from either side and the opportunity for families to dine away from the rowdy crowd in the public bar. That, coupled with the fact he had no decent food on his menu, drove his urge to make the change.

Plus, he hated the deep fryers.

Stepping behind the bar, Luke reached for a cloth and settled in for a busy night. He pulled beers, mixed spirits, and scooped ice for soft drinks. A couple of young girls flirted with him as he popped open cans of vodka, but since they were just of legal age to sit in his pub, he smiled politely and moved toward the bistro bar. He might be nearing thirty but unfortunately, he hardly had time for women. They rarely stuck around when he worked most nights, which was a damn shame as he enjoyed dating and planned to settle down one day. He might not be in a hurry to do so, but it had been a long time since he'd had a woman to spend time with. To talk to and love. Spoil. Cherish.

Which he was frustratingly reminded of when Grace White walked through the glass doors and into the bistro.

Luke's hand tightened around the dishcloth as a strange warmth filled his chest. It had been happening a lot lately when she was around, but he couldn't put his finger on why. He'd known Grace all his life and sure, he liked her. She was a kind, generous woman who wasn't afraid to go after what she wanted. She wasn't an exceptional beauty, but pretty in a plain way with a splatter of freckles across her nose and hair a caramel brown. Yet her chocolatey eyes always sparkled and tonight, her short red lace dress highlighted her masterful yoga-toned legs.

Luke swallowed and tore his gaze away as he scanned the bistro for her colleagues. But she was the first of the Elizadale Medical team to arrive.

'Hey, Luke.' Grace smiled as she leaned her forearms on

the lacquered wooden bar and interlocked her slender fingers. His pulse stupidly quickened.

'How's it going, Grace?'

'All right. I guess I'm the first one here.'

'I haven't seen your colleagues. Can I get you a drink?'

'Yes, a Diet Coke, please.'

He grabbed a can from the fridge beneath the bar and scooped a glass of ice, but before he could make conversation, Emma Knight arrived and called Grace's name.

'Thanks, Luke.' Smiling softly, she lifted her drink from the bar and turned as Emma approached. The ladies hugged and complimented each other on their outfits, then Emma ordered a vodka. After running through the transaction, Luke watched the nurses cross the bistro towards their table, his gaze glued to Grace's swaying hips until the dishwasher beeped, reminding him he had a job to do.

Shaking his head at himself, Luke unloaded the glasses and slid the tray into the rack, ready to use. He set another load to wash, then turned to the main bar where he served drinks and chatted with locals as though they were his friends. But the image of Grace sashaying towards her table in her little red dress continued to plague his mind. Twisting the top off a bottle of Great Northern beer, he wished the replay would stop. It wasn't the first time he'd seen her in a dress that had knocked him for six. If anyone in Elizadale regularly wore fancy dresses to the pub, it was his sister and her friends.

Jessica's laugh cut through the chatter and he watched as she served a bunch of young blokes. He made change for the beer, served another whiskey, then the back of his neck prickled. Glancing towards the bistro bar, he found Grace waiting patiently. A soft smile curved her mouth and his heart flipped.

'Another Diet Coke?' Not that he needed to ask. She didn't drink anything else.

'Yes, please. Looks like you're doing well tonight.'

'Fridays are always busy.' He placed the drink on the bar and took her money. 'Need to make the most of them.'

'Absolutely. I saw the chef's special tonight is vegetarian lasagne. That's not one of the usuals. Is it any good?'

'I hope so. I've asked Bill to try new dishes to see how the locals like them.'

Her eyebrows shot up. 'That sounds like a great idea.'

Luke stilled. 'Yeah?'

'Absolutely. I mean, no offence, but the menu here hasn't changed since we were kids.'

'Exactly! And it's all boring, crap food.'

She laughed and Luke's heart swelled until he could barely breathe. 'Hey, you're the one who said it. But a change sounds good, Luke. I could taste the Caesar salad just looking at the menu, so I'm glad there was something different. I'll let you know how the lasagne is.'

He tried and failed to contain his grin. 'I look forward to your opinion.'

Grace turned, the ends of her hair lifting and swishing over her shoulders. Luke watched her go as she strolled to the table with the red lace clinging to her body. She liked his idea and wanted new food. Hopefully, that meant other people would too.

Although suddenly, Grace's opinion seemed to be the only one that mattered.

Luke exhaled and placed his hands on the bar. Shit.

Chapter Three

Grace resumed her seat beside Emma at the table as she and her colleagues celebrated the end of the year with their Christmas party. She and Emma made up the nursing staff of Elizadale Medical and were good friends since they'd known each other all their lives. Some days, Grace could hardly believe they worked together for Doctor Joanne Brennan, who'd been Elizadale's general practitioner since before she and Emma had been born. Such was the beauty of small towns.

Joanne chatted with her husband, David, and the pharmacist, James, while their receptionist, Nikki, was at the bar with James' two assistants.

'So, how'd it go with your family?' Emma asked.

Grace's mouth twisted. 'I shouldn't have expected much. You know that guy I met at the rodeo?'

'Matt?'

'He invited me to visit him for Christmas but knowing that he probably wants more from me than presents, I told him no. Dad's beside himself. He wants me to marry Matt.'

Emma rolled her eyes. 'What does he think this is? The Nineteenth Century? Fourteenth?'

'I know, right? I don't need that right now. The yoga studio is my priority.'

Emma beamed. 'I'm so excited about that. So is Mum.'

'That's awesome.' Emma's mum, Linda, was a school-teacher and would undoubtedly spread the word. 'Of course, Dad thinks I'm wasting my time, but I know I can pull it off.'

'You will. Don't worry about that.'

'Thanks.' Grace slumped into her seat. 'But I still wish I had Mum and Dad's support. You'd think parents would be impressed about their kid starting their own business. But even my mum wants me barefoot and pregnant.'

'Yeah …' Emma sipped her vodka. 'Your parents sure are something.'

'Yep. Almost makes me want to swear off men just to spite them.'

'Don't do that! You can't deny yourself that fun.'

'I know, but I think it might be why I've avoided dating these past few months.' Apart from her stupid interlude with Matt, she hadn't dated for more than a year.

'Do you want to date?'

Grace shook her head. 'It's not worth the risk. He'd have to own a hell of a lot of land otherwise Dad would try to break us up.'

'Fathers, right? I think the only reason Ian and I started dating was because it took me six months to tell him Dad was a copper.'

Grace smiled. 'Yeah, but I think Ian would have dated you anyway. You two are like a fairy tale, love at first sight and married since the tenth grade.'

'We've been *together* since the tenth grade. But honestly,

Grace, don't let fear of what your parents think stop you from going after what you want.'

'I'm not! This yoga studio is going to happen.'

Emma rolled her eyes. 'I mean with dating.'

'Oh. Right.'

'Get out there and check out the blokes. There are quite a few hotties in town.'

'But I've known most of them my whole life. How do you bridge the gap from friends or acquaintances to … more?'

'If you both want it badly enough, shouldn't it just happen?'

'Good thing I don't want it that badly then.'

Emma quirked her eyebrow. 'Don't you?'

'Maybe,' Grace winced. 'I might have a shot if people could keep a damn secret in this town, then Dad would never know. But it's impossible, Emma.' Any man who took an interest in her would only end up hurt.

'Your dad may be hard, Grace, but most of the blokes our age know that.'

Grace sighed. She didn't want to think about this. Tonight was supposed to be fun. A party. Nikki, Holly, and Jenna were certainly enjoying themselves as they giggled over their bottle of wine. So Grace indulged her friend. 'Then who would you suggest?'

Emma pursed her lips. 'Well … I saw Darren yesterday when he serviced my car. He's a hottie.'

Grace nodded. Darren Hudson was a mechanic with broad shoulders, large hands, and he looked sexy covered in grease. 'Yeah, but he's Adam's friend. In this town, you can't date an ex's friends. Or brothers.'

'Well, that sure narrows it down. I was going to mention Cade.'

Grace laughed. 'You'd pimp out your own brother?'

'I don't think he'd mind.'

That was true. Cade Wilson had once been quite the rebel, enjoyed women, and was Adam Maguire's partner in crime. But since Cade had returned from the police academy a few years ago, he'd been a respectable citizen who was passionate about the law and doing the right thing.

Would her father dare try to intimidate and run off a copper?

'He might not mind,' Grace agreed, 'but he's into Jessica. And she's crushing hard on him. I can't do that to my best friend.'

'Tell me about it. I hear about Jessica every time I speak to him.' Her face turned serious. 'What about Luke?'

Grace's eyebrows shot up. 'Luke?'

Emma nodded across the room and Grace studied Luke Smithfield as he served a young family, cheer in his smile of straight teeth and a sparkle in his bright blue eyes. He wore his dark hair spikey at the top and shorter at the sides, and people behaved in his pub because nobody wanted to see his square jaw tense and eyes flame. But mostly, they behaved because Luke was *built*. His Smithfield Hotel polo clung to every swell and groove of his hard chest, broad shoulders, and his sleeves almost burst at the seams.

Frowning, Grace turned back to Emma. 'No … like I said. Jessica's my best friend. I couldn't date her brother.'

'Why not? People fall in love with friend's siblings all the time.'

Grace choked on her drink. 'I'm not looking to fall in love!'

'You say that now.' Emma waved Grace's protest away with her hand. 'But you *can* open a yoga studio and fall in love too, you know?'

Unease swirled in her belly. 'Yeah … but …'

Emma grinned. 'I'd like to see your dad try to scare off Luke.'

Grace's heart leapt. That would be a sight indeed. Luke was the most determined and confident man she knew. No one told Luke what to do. No one.

'Business wise, it makes sense. Doesn't it, Grace?'

Blinking at the sound of her name, Grace turned to Joanne. 'Sorry, what was that?'

'Getting a new doctor.'

'Oh, yes.' She smiled and glanced between David and James. 'A registrar will take a lot of weight off Joanne as well as bring extra funding to the business. We could really use that this year.'

While she might be only qualified as a nurse, Grace had taken on a managerial role at Elizadale Medical and handled many of the business aspects. It'd been two years since their last registrar left and while the practice could run with Joanne alone, it certainly thrived with two doctors. Not to mention the extra help would allow Joanne to take some well-deserved time off.

'We will advertise early in the year,' Joanne said.

'And don't forget about the new nurse,' Emma said. '*Temp* nurse. For my maternity leave.'

Laughing softly, Grace placed her hand on Emma's forearm. 'You have to *get* pregnant first.'

'Just giving you fair warning. Naomi's eighteen months old and it's time she became a big sister.'

As baby talk grasped the attention of Nikki, Holly, and Jenna, Grace sipped her drink and listened in. She was happy for her friend, who enjoyed her cosy family life, but babies weren't on Grace's radar just yet. One day, probably. But as she listened to the ladies gush about babies and weddings, Grace's thoughts drifted back to what Emma had said.

Grace had been holding back in her own love life. It was easy to do in the face of inevitable defeat. Why risk her father's wrath and her own heart when it'd been broken so many times before?

Her gaze wandered from her friends towards the bar where it landed on Luke Smithfield. He was a nice man and she'd known him a long time. And even though he'd never been anything to her other than Jessica's brother and the man who served her drinks, she wouldn't deny he was pleasing to look at. She didn't go to Elizadale football games with her friends because she liked rugby league. Most of the girls went to perv and the image of Luke in his tight jersey, short shorts, and grass stains on his strong thighs …

'The lasagne?'

Grace glanced at the waitress delivering their meals. 'Thank you,' she said, her stomach rumbling. Food was just what she needed to stop her crazy thoughts.

Studying the meal, it certainly looked appetising with the pasta sitting perfectly stacked, the tomatoey sauce seeping out the sides while the bechamel glistened on top with a sprinkle of herbs and cheese. Breathing in the rich aroma, Grace sliced into the lasagne, popped the first bite into her mouth, and almost moaned as the garlic mixed with the mushroom, eggplant, and spinach. Nothing had ever tasted more divine.

Luke should definitely put this on the regular menu.

Her colleagues continued to chat throughout dinner, discussing their plans for Christmas. No one was going anywhere or doing anything special, nor was Elizadale Medical closing except on the public holidays. But Grace hardly joined in the merriment as they talked about their families since she had nothing to be excited about. Every year she tried to enjoy the day to no avail, and usually left her parents' house feeling dejected, wishing she could have spent the day alone or with her friends.

But suggesting that would only infuriate her parents more.

Grace polished off her lasagne, savouring every bite, and once their plates were cleared, they took advantage of the dessert special. When their pavlovas were served, Grace helped herself to Emma's discarded strawberries and indulged in the sugary sweetness of the meringue.

She'd just scooped the last crumb up with her finger when Jessica arrived at her side.

'Hey, Jess. How was your night?'

'Busy, but things are quieting down, so Luke's sending me home. Thought I'd stop by and say hello. I hope you all enjoyed your evening.'

'It was wonderful, Jessica,' Joanne replied with a smile. 'Thank you.'

'No worries.' Jessica turned to Grace. 'I'll see you in the morning, yeah?'

Grace nodded. She and Jessica lived with their other friend, Claire, and they were driving to Cairns tomorrow for Christmas shopping. 'Yep. Will I need to drag you out of bed?'

'Nah, I'll be right.'

Grace and Jessica said their goodbyes, then a short while later, their party made a move. Grace picked up her bag and was about to join Emma and Nikki when she stopped.

'Actually, ladies. I might stay a moment.'

Emma's gaze darted over Grace's shoulder. 'Ah. I see,' she said, a twinkle filling her eyes.

'Don't look at me like that, Em,' Grace said. 'I just want to tell Luke what I thought about dinner. He wants to revamp the menu.'

'If you say so.' Emma's smile didn't waver as she lifted her hand in farewell. 'Have a nice night.'

Ignoring her friend, Grace waved her off, then crossed the room and pulled open the door to the public bar. Kenny Rogers played on the jukebox and balls clattered on the pool table as two old blokes started a game. Other patrons continued to linger while Tina and Luke worked the bar.

Grace's hand tightened around her handbag. Shit, he was hot. Why hadn't she ever acknowledged that before? She'd known the man for-almost-ever!

Shaking it off, she shoved Emma's annoying little voice out of her head. She wasn't interested in Luke like that. She wanted to know more about his menu idea because while she liked food and didn't mind cooking, sometimes she wasn't in the mood. And she wouldn't mind having a nice place to eat. A place that wouldn't clog her arteries and pound on the kilos with its deep friend junk. If Luke could give her that, then she wanted to help.

Taking a deep breath, Grace strode to the bar and sat.

Chapter Four

As Luke lifted a tray of glasses from the dishwasher, his gaze locked with Grace's and his heart buckled. Shit. What was with that?

'How was your night?' he asked.

'Lovely. We all had a good time, but I have to say, the lasagne was a-*ma*-zing!'

He grinned. 'Excellent. I'm glad you liked it.'

'Oh, I did. It was delicious, well presented, and just the right size.'

'I'll tell Bill.' He turned to the fridge and grabbed a can of Diet Coke. 'For you. On the house.'

'Oh.' Her long lashes blinked rapidly as she curled her delicate hand around the can. 'Thank you.'

'Thank you for your feedback.' He scooped her a glass of ice. 'I'm super keen to update the menu, but not everyone will be, so I need all the support I can get.'

'Why don't you think people will be keen?'

'Change is hard to accept for some people and I don't just want to add a new dish or two. I want to throw out the clichéd pub classics and aim for something more gourmet.'

Grace's red mouth curved as she poured the Coke over the ice. 'Sounds good. It'll certainly help you stand out. We don't have great dining out options in town.'

His shoulders loosened as he reached for the glasses and continued to clean up. 'Exactly. I mean, we'll keep the steaks and some classics, but I like the idea of changing the lasagne because we should have a vegetarian option.'

She nodded. 'I prefer the vegetarian option. It has more flavour and a melt-in-your-mouth quality. Plus, I don't eat beef.'

Luke paused in setting the dishwasher and glanced at her over his shoulder. 'You don't?'

'Nope.' Her dark hair swished as she shook her head.

'But … you grew up on a cattle farm.'

'Exactly! I've seen what happens to those cows and my father's practices are far worse than other farmers who are keeping up with the times. I know other meat isn't raised any better, but at least when I have chicken or fish on my plate, I don't have images of their short lives flashing through my mind.'

'Fair enough.' He set the dishwasher and straightened. 'I didn't realise your dad was like that.'

'Don't get me started,' she muttered. Irritation flashed through her eyes, then she shook her head and smiled. 'But yes, the vegetarian lasagne is a must for the new menu. What else do you have in mind?'

He had so many ideas he didn't know where to start. 'What about herb-encrusted salmon?'

Her eyebrows lifted. 'Yum.'

'And maybe coconut chicken on pineapple fried rice.'

'Now you're making me hungry. I love coconut rice.'

He shook his head. 'Not coconut rice. Yes, it's delicious,

but I'm thinking a coconut sauce on the chicken with pineapple and vegetables in the rice. I know it usually goes the other way around, but trust me, it's good.'

'I don't doubt it. The whole idea sounds exciting.'

Smiling, Luke leaned his hip on the back bar opposite her and crossed his arms over his chest. 'I hope so. People will come to check it out at least once.'

'Fill it with variety and they'll come back multiple times to try everything.'

'Very true. Bill's partially on board, but he's not sure if it's a smart idea to take chicken schnitzel off the menu.'

Her creamy brow furrowed. 'Why would you want chicken schnitzel when you can have coconut chicken on rice?'

'Exactly!' At least she understood.

'Well, I hope you bring Bill around, Luke. I'm sure it'll be a success. I'm just surprised Jessica hasn't said anything to me. Is she on your side?'

'I only mentioned it to her this afternoon, but you know Jess. She rarely expresses a negative opinion, so she reckons I should give it a shot.' Straightening, Luke reached for his abandoned dishcloth. 'She said you guys are going to Cairns in the morning.'

'Yeah, we need some things for Christmas. Especially decorations. We're putting up lights at Jackson Villas tomorrow and Claire wanted something to hang in the windows.'

'Sounds like fun. Do you need any help?'

She shook her head. 'We always do it together. But I'm sure Jess will call if she needs you.'

Luke loaded another tray of glasses. 'I doubt Jessica would call anyone for help, but I'll stop by to see your lights.'

Grace smiled around her straw, and the insane knotting returned to his stomach. 'Thanks. I doubt we'll beat Margaret Riley's famous display. None of us has the time for that. But we'll do our best. What are you doing for Christmas?'

Luke shrugged. 'The usual, I guess. I'll join Mum, Dad, and Jess at church in the morning.'

'I thought you didn't go to church.'

'I don't normally, but I go on Christmas and Easter to please Mum.' Luke might have been raised a Christian, but while he still held some of those values close to his heart, he'd fallen out of the routine of regular church attendance after leaving home. 'She always does a good job with lunch, then Dad and I will probably get in some practice for the Boxing Day test.'

Grace laughed. 'Of course.'

Every year, the men of Elizadale gathered on Boxing Day for a game of cricket. They might be a small town, but they loved their community sport and Luke invested himself in the rugby league, cricket, and soccer teams. For decades, Elizadale had hosted a cricket game on Boxing Day morning and locals of all ages joined in.

'What about you?' he asked. 'Any big Christmas plans?'

'Not really.' Her gaze dropped as she swirled the ice in her glass. 'Same as always with lunch on the station. I'm not sure what Charlie and Zoe are going to do, but they'll spend part of the day with her family.'

The joy in her eyes vanished at the mention of her family, and Luke frowned. Not much went unnoticed in a town as small as Elizadale and he'd spent most of his life inside the gossipy walls of the local watering hole. Edward and Francesca White were not popular and few locals had anything pleasant to say about them. It had been that way since well before Luke had been born, back when White Peaks had fallen out of favour with the other farmers after Edward's father had been charged with fraud and theft.

But Luke didn't care much about the past. All he knew was that Grace wasn't a liar like her father and grandfather.

And that she looked beautiful in red.

'I guess, as a family, we're lucky there,' he said. 'It's still just the four of us. But it won't always be like that.'

'No. Families do grow.'

He nodded slowly, then before he could stop himself, he asked, 'Are you seeing anyone at the moment?'

The ice stopped tinkling in her drink as she lifted her gaze to his. 'No. What about you?'

The dishwasher pinged, and Luke straightened. 'Nope.'

Unloading the glasses, his heart pounded a drum against his ribs. He slid in the next tray, glanced back at her, and stilled. Her red, glossy, almost sinful lips moved ever so slightly as she chewed on her straw. Would they taste as good as they looked? Feel that soft against his own?

She placed her glass back on the bar, thumping him out of his fantasies. 'So, when do you start football training again?'

'The season doesn't start until April, so we won't begin formal training until March,' he replied, moving about as he continued to pack up. 'Unless Joe wants to get a head start on things and run us into the ground.' His good mate and team captain Joe Cooper was the local physical education teacher, a hardcore footy coach, and brutal fitness trainer. Not that Luke minded as he loved pushing his body to its physical limits. 'It's not too serious, you know?'

'I guess not, but it's still fun. We girls like going.'

'Yeah, I usually see you there.'

Her lips curved. 'We need to do something to keep our weekends interesting.'

Warmth spread through his chest as her eyes glittered, but before Luke could reply, Tina arrived with one of the tills.

'I've settled this one, Luke. Bob and Roy are heading off after this game of pool, so I can finish cleaning up.'

Luke liked Tina. She was a nice young woman and a fantastic worker. But at this very moment, he wasn't pleased about being interrupted.

'Okay. I'll take this till and you can settle the other one.'

Even though the pub was closed, Luke still had paperwork to take care of. But as he tucked the till against his hip, he didn't want to end his time with Grace. Not now. He enjoyed talking to her and it wasn't yet midnight. So as Tina wandered off, Luke swallowed the knot in his throat and took a shot.

'Come out back with me, Grace.'

* * *

Grace's eyebrows shot up. She'd thought Luke was finishing for the evening and that she should be going home. But by the look in his deep blue eyes, it seemed like he didn't want her to go anywhere. Nor did she wish to end their conversation.

She grabbed her glass, left the empty can, and stood. 'Okay.'

Luke smiled softly and strode out from behind the bar. Ignoring her racing heart, Grace followed him through the pub as her gaze wandered from his wide shoulders and down the V of his torso. His butt looked damn good in those jeans, as did his strong thighs straining against the denim. It might be common for some men who enjoyed weight-training to neglect their lower body and focus on enhancing their pecs and bulging their biceps, but not Luke. He was the whole package.

Luke fished the keys from his pocket and unlocked the door, leading her through the hallway and into one of the two offices.

He gestured towards the chairs. 'Have a seat.'

Not sure why she was there anymore, Grace sat and placed her drink on the edge of the desk. She didn't bother looking around as she'd been in the office plenty of times with Jessica, but the room held a far greater presence with Luke's broad shoulders behind the desk.

Crossing her legs, Grace forced her spine to soften. 'So … do you bring girls back here often?'

He paused counting ten-dollar bills and lifted his eyes to hers. 'No,' he said, then resumed counting.

Grace watched his large hands shift through the blue notes. Damn, even his hands were appealing. At the bar, his impressive biceps had mesmerised her as he'd lifted heavy trays from the dishwasher. To partially conceal them beneath sleeves was a travesty, but to expose them would be torture to the female population.

She turned her gaze to the wall and sipped her drink. What was wrong with her? She didn't want to be checking out Luke Smithfield. That was a dangerous game that would undoubtedly end in tears. Her father would never approve and she wasn't interested in dating. All she'd wanted was to chat about his new menu, but the conversation had veered and now she was alone with him.

Grace's heart pounded hard and low. Tina arrived with the second till and left without a word, closing the door behind her. As Luke finished the first till, he placed it on the bench behind him and Grace hastened to fill the silence.

'What desserts are you going to serve?'

A small smile curved Luke's mouth as he stood. 'I have some ideas. I'd like to highlight local produce, so I've considered coffee and banana desserts.'

Grace's spine softened. 'They're our two biggest exports, and there's plenty you could do with both.'

'I thought a banana split would go down well.'

Luke stacked the tills on top of each other and crouched to open the safe. Grace nodded slowly, biting her lip as her gaze wandered up his back and shoulders.

'You could make it a feature dessert,' she said as she stood, needing to move. 'Maybe provide a variety of flavour toppings. Or a build-your-own.'

'I could do that. I also want to expand the coffee menu, especially on the alcoholic side of things.'

'Irish coffee can be a popular dessert.'

'What about coffee with Bailey's Irish Crème?'

He turned and flashed her a smile. Grace clutched the edge of the desk. Good God, why were her knees weakening over Luke? What was she doing alone in his office with him when everything inside her was burning?

'Jessica likes Bailey's,' she replied.

'She does.' He slipped his hands into his pockets and Grace sank onto the edge of the desk. 'So, why don't you drink?'

He asked with interest, not a hint of judgement in his eyes.

Grace licked her dry lips and let out a small breath. 'Dad's a mean drunk. He relies too much on alcohol and sometimes gets a little …' She paused on the word 'violent'. Few people knew what went on inside the walls of the White Peaks homestead and she didn't want to broadcast it. 'Mean. Besides, I don't like the taste and it ruins perfectly good soft drink.'

'Fair enough. So …' His gaze dropped as he scratched the back of his head. 'You seem keen on the new menu idea.'

'Yeah …'

'Then what do you think about helping me out?' His eyes met hers again. 'See, Bill's more of a cook than a chef and not very creative. Neither am I, really, but if I want to make the changes, I need to come up with the ideas. And Bill can cook anything with instructions, so I want to test some dishes out and if you want to come over for dinner on Sunday …'

Grace's heart pounded as she studied Luke shifting his feet with his hands in his pockets. Was he nervous? Was he asking her out? Or did he just want her help as a friend?

Dammit, if Emma hadn't put stupid thoughts into her head, she wouldn't have to ask herself such questions.

'I'd love to help you, Luke. I can come over on Sunday.'

In fact, it sounded like just what she needed. Grace hadn't realised it until Emma had mentioned dating, but she might have been a little lonely lately. And while she had a lot on her plate with work and preparing to start her yoga classes, creating a menu with Luke might spark some joy during the depressing Christmas season.

'Excellent.' Luke's grin lit up his face. 'It should be fun, I think.'

'It will be,' she agreed, grinning in return. 'So, what do you want me to taste test first?'

He shrugged and pushed off the wall. 'What would you like?'

He moved towards her and she caught a whiff of his

woodsy scent. Unfortunately, it was tainted with the stench of beer, which wasn't surprising, but otherwise …

'I like vegetables. And if you want a fresh menu, I think your focus should be there. With stir-fries, pastas, and salads.'

'I agree. And I'll serve the meats with vegetables and baked potato.'

'Sounds good,' she breathed. He stood so close. 'Chips and salad are boring.'

'And overdone.'

'And I prefer restaurants that serve vegetables.'

'Me too.' His gaze dropped to her shoulders, then ran down her body before quickly lifting back to hers. Grace's heart leapt. Was it just her or did their talk of food create more sizzle than the kitchen? Did Luke feel it too? Would flames erupt between them if she were to grab him by the collar and press her mouth to his?

Luke stepped back and cleared his throat. 'It's getting late. I should let you go.'

Grace jumped off the desk like it had zapped her. 'Yeah. And I have an early start.'

'I'll walk you out.'

She grabbed her bag from the floor, then followed Luke out of the office. Striding through the dark pub, Grace shoved aside her wayward thoughts. She didn't want to kiss Luke. She didn't want to run her hands up his body and fuel their fire.

Her father would burn them alive.

'How's seven on Sunday?' Luke asked, opening the door to the carpark.

Grace nodded. It might be a stupid idea, but she'd offered to help and wouldn't go back on her word. 'Seven's perfect.'

Chapter Five

'It's been forever since we were in Cairns,' Jessica said as they left Elizadale the following morning. 'It'll be nice to shop without paying for shipping. I'm in desperate need of the last few seasons of *Heartland*. And art supplies.'

'Tell me about it,' Claire agreed. 'At least I can read on Kindle these days, but we should go to town more often.'

'And I could do with some new shoes. My joggers are hurting my feet.'

'Mine too. Grace, what do you need?'

Comfortable in the back of Claire's car, Grace stared out the window as they drove past Shadow Creek. She couldn't stop thinking about last night and the foolish desire to kiss Luke, but at Claire's question, she snapped back into reality and glanced at her friends.

'I have to pick up the yoga flyers I printed, but you know me. I'll buy a bunch of clothes that I don't need.'

Claire laughed. 'But that's what a shopping spree is all about!'

'I'm getting a new dress for Christmas Day,' Jessica said, turning in the passenger seat. 'But let's not go overboard.'

Grace rolled her eyes. 'Speak for yourself! We work hard and deserve to spoil ourselves.'

The drive from Elizadale to Cairns took just under two hours. They passed through the country town of Mareeba, where they usually shopped for the basics, then drove down the range to the coastal tourist hotspot of Cairns. Grace grinned as the city vibe closed in around her. She loved shopping with her friends and was glad to have escaped the country for the day. There were no two people that Grace valued more than Jessica and Claire. She might be a year younger than them, which had made things difficult at school, but they had shared every moment growing up together. Jessica was a town girl and had worked at the Smithfield Hotel since she was fourteen, happy to settle there with a regular wage while she pursued her true passion for acrylic painting. Claire had grown up a farm girl like Grace, the youngest of three children from Tropic Sun banana farm, but she too had desired town life and was now the beloved local hairdresser.

But while Jessica might be one of her best friends, Grace couldn't bring herself to tell her that Luke was cooking her dinner tomorrow. Not when she couldn't get this sizzle under control. Besides, Jessica would ask too many questions that Grace wouldn't have an answer for, so it was best she didn't say anything at all.

They stopped at Officeworks and Grace collected the flyers and business cards she'd ordered. Having designed them herself, with the help of online software, they looked fabulous with hot pink swirls surrounding a cartoon figure in a lotus pose.

'I'll take some into the salon and spread the word,' Claire said as they returned to the car. 'When are you going to distribute?'

'Monday after work. And Joanne said I can place business cards on the reception desk, so hopefully I'll get some takers.'

'I wouldn't worry, Grace,' Jessica said. 'People love you, so they'll come to try yoga.'

Grace could only hope as they arrived at Cairns Central, though she had a good feeling. They leapt out of the car and a spring filled Grace's step as she entered the brightly lit hall filled with Christmas decorations, bustling shoppers, and carols playing overhead. Approaching Forever New, Grace's gaze fell on the red bodycon dress and her heart swooned. Oh, she was in trouble. 'Tis the season to wear red, her favourite colour, and the dress was on sale.

'That is so you, Grace,' Jessica said, as they entered the store. 'You'll look hot in that.'

Grinning, Grace reached for her size. 'I doubt I can leave it behind.'

'Absolutely not. And do you see all that pink over there? My bank account is going to weep.'

'We only come to town every few months,' Claire reminded them and with that, they gathered all the pretty dresses that tickled their fancy and skipped into the change rooms.

Pulling the red dress up her lean body, Grace glanced at herself in the mirror and grinned. Oh, yes. With her tanned skin and dark hair, she was a knockout in red and thanks to her dedicated yoga practice, she had the body to pull off the clinging bodycon style. Maybe she could wear this dress to dinner tomorrow?

Her heart stuttered. No, that would send the wrong message. She was *not* interested in dating Luke or making his mouth water.

'How are you going?' Jessica called out.

'I love this!' Claire said.

'Oh, it's so cute!'

Grace poked her head out of the dressing room to see Claire twirling in a blue babydoll. 'I like it,' she agreed.

'Show us yours!' Jessica said, and she gasped when Grace stepped out of the room. 'I love it.'

'Super sexy,' Claire agreed.

'You're getting it, right?' Jessica asked.

Laughing, Grace turned side on and stared at herself in the mirror. 'Absolutely.'

She bought three dresses, then they continued through the shopping centre, trying on clothes, ogling jewellery, and treating themselves to anything they wanted. But Grace struggled with buying for others as gift giving wasn't her forte. Jessica and Claire found great presents for their parents, siblings, and—in Claire's case—nieces, but Grace relied on her sister-in-law's suggestions and bought a few things she could address to both her parents, so at least she wouldn't show up on Christmas Day empty handed. Then they found the decorations, chose a few flashing lights, and headed home to deck the halls of their townhouse.

* * *

They returned late afternoon to the units Grace and her friends had called home these past few years. Jackson Villas consisted of five double-storey townhouses built of pale-yellow brick and since women also occupied the other units, they'd formed their own little community and spent the time before sunset decorating. It wasn't any cooler, but at least the sun didn't scorch their skin as they lined candy cane stakes in the garden and wrapped lights around the post. They even decorated unit five's patio with the help of the current tenant, but sadly, Tiffany wouldn't be there for Christmas. Like many blow-ins, she had spent a year teaching at the school and was returning home to the city.

Once darkness had fallen, they'd switched on the lights and stood on the footpath to admire their handiwork. Grace smiled. She loved Christmas. It might be boiling beneath the ferocity of the North Queensland sun, but she enjoyed the festivities around town and celebrating with her friends. Christmas Day itself wasn't anything special since her family gatherings hardly had the potential to be warm and cosy, but at least she had these ladies and her friends at work.

After profusely thanking everyone for their efforts, Grace and her friends farewelled their neighbours and headed inside their unit, number two, to continue decorating. Claire set up her new Bluetooth speaker, hit play on her Spotify playlist, and they set up their artificial tree beneath the running air conditioner as 'Winter Wonderland' filled the room with Christmas cheer.

'If only we had snow,' Jessica sighed from her position at the coffee table where she sat arranging candle centrepieces.

Claire shuddered. 'No thanks. But your candles look good, Jess.'

'I know, right?'

Grace glanced at the candle centrepiece Jessica had created. A red pillar candle stood between two shorter green ones in a bowl of gold tinsel and plastic holly.

'Where are you going to put the ceramic reindeer?' Grace asked, reaching for the frosted pink ornaments as the song changed to the more upbeat 'Rocking Around the Christmas Tree'. Claire's kelpie, Maggie, uncurled herself from her pillow in the corner, her toenails clipping on the tiles as she wandered over.

'With some yellow candles on the table among green tinsel so it looks like grass.'

Grace laughed as Maggie inspected the candles with a sniff. 'Sounds nice. Are we going to wrap tinsel around the staircase?'

'We can do that when we finish the tree.' Placing the ice blue ornaments, Claire glanced at Grace. 'Oh, I haven't asked, how was the Christmas party last night?'

Heat rose in her cheeks and Grace bent down to place the larger baubles on the lower branches. 'It was good. I had the most delicious vegetarian lasagne.'

'Vegetarian?' Claire sounded surprised.

'Yeah,' Jessica said. 'Luke's trying new dishes because he wants to change the menu, so I'll tell him you liked it, Grace. He's keen for feedback.'

'That's okay.' Grace tucked hair behind her ear and made a show out of gathering more ornaments. 'I mentioned it to him before I left.'

'Was it busy?' Claire asked, this question directed at Jessica.

'Always, which is good because Luke's worried that we're down on revenue.' Jessica stood from the coffee table and joined them at the tree. Maggie dashed over and inspected the lower ornaments, her curious nose twitching.

'Really?' Grace asked. 'Is Smithy's in trouble?'

'We could be doing better, but it's nothing to worry about. And Luke's right, the menu hasn't changed in years. It'll draw people in just out of curiosity.'

'But what about the new café at the Tourist Centre?' Claire asked, shooing Maggie away from the tree. 'Liam Maguire's opening that soon and plans to have a fresh, diverse menu. Is now a good time for Smithy's to do the same?'

'The café won't open until Easter,' Grace said. 'And Liam's aiming for a different clientele.'

'And he won't be open for dinner,' Jessica added, 'so I don't think there'll be an issue. But there's a lot of new things to look forward to this coming year. Like Grace's yoga class.'

Grateful for the change of subject, Grace clipped silver butterflies to the tree. 'It's going to be great, and at least I won't need to drive to Mareeba every week. That's if people come, anyway.'

'They'll come. And I've already told Luke that I won't be able to work Thursday nights.' Jessica stepped back from the tree and admired their handiwork. 'Yep, I think we did a good job.'

'I love the pink, blue, and silver,' Claire said, rubbing Maggie's head as the chocolate kelpie glanced up at the tree with a sparkle in her dark eyes.

'It's a pretty change from the red and gold,' Grace agreed. 'Well, dinner should be ready, so I'll grab that. Then we can do the tinsel.'

Grace microwaved peas and carrots, then divvied up the oven-baked homemade chips and frozen fish before sitting at their small dining table. Claire ruined her chips with a smothering of tomato sauce, but Grace and Jessica tucked into theirs as they were.

'Jingle Bells' started playing as Claire said, 'So, my family is buying an above ground pool for Christmas, which will be fun. Faith and Lisa will love it.'

'I think you'll love it more,' Grace said, imagining Claire acting like a big kid and splashing around with her nieces.

Jessica shook her head. 'I don't understand why none of you farming families have pools.'

'I know.' Grace had wished for a pool while growing up, but of course, such things cost money and she'd had to make do with the dam a three kilometre walk away. 'The Kellys have one, but it wasn't worth risking a friendship with Jordan for.'

Claire's nose crinkled. 'I know. She was almost tolerable in primary school and I did swim in that pool a bit. But ever since high school, I can't stand the woman.'

Grace nodded as she scooped up her peas. Her family hadn't been friends with the Kellys, unlike Claire's, but most people in town had a reason to dislike Jordan Kelly. For Grace, it was the fact she'd tried to steal Adam from her when they'd been dating, as Jordan was predatory like that. But Adam hadn't strayed, even though he and Jordan had history.

'Me neither,' Jessica agreed, glancing at Grace. 'And speaking of men, I can't believe Matt invited you to spend Christmas with him.'

'It wasn't his idea,' Grace muttered. 'Dad had a hand in it and is pissed that I'm not going. Practically called me a slut too for sleeping with Matt.'

Claire slapped her hand on the table. 'Oh my God!'

'How does *he* know you slept with him?'

'I don't want to know. He wants us together, and it wouldn't surprise me if he's keeping tabs on his schemes. Which is why I'm pissed off that I fell for it and slept with Matt.'

Claire placed her hand on Grace's forearm. 'A woman's entitled to have fun,' Claire reminded her, as she always did when Grace expressed her regret. 'You have nothing to be ashamed of.'

'I know, but I hate how Dad thinks he can hold it over me. Not that I'm surprised.'

Yet she couldn't help the anger that coursed through her as she stabbed at a chip. If her father was capable of a reasonable conversation, then they'd be able to settle their differences and find common ground. She could feel like she had a family. And while she might not receive love, she might be granted a smidgen of respect.

Grace choked back a laugh. Edward White would never change. She'd learned that when he hadn't attended her university graduation.

Chapter Six

Edward White's hand tightened around his whiskey glass. That daughter of his had some nerve. And no brains. Stupid girl had always been naïve, off with the fairies, and had no interest in doing what was best for herself or her family.

How the hell had he raised such a selfish child?

The phone rang and Edward snatched it up. 'White Peaks.'

'Your daughter has turned me down. Again.' Matt Clark's irritation rippled down the phone line. 'I thought we had a deal, White.'

'And I thought you had everything settled.' Edward tossed back his whiskey, refusing to let Matt blame him for his own lack of game. The man might have learned how to do business just as well as his father—and Richard Clark didn't continue to build on his wealth because he was nice—but Matt was just a kid. And Edward wouldn't let some kid who'd had the world laid at his polished boots intimidate him. 'I thought you'd won Grace over in August, so how was I supposed to know she'd reject your invitation?'

'Then tell her to change her mind. I'll be living at Redback permanently come the New Year and my father will give me more control of the empire if I find myself a wife. Grace is a good catch and, as promised, if we form this union between our properties, then you can use my Wagyu bull, Wally, at the discounted fee.'

Edward's hand tightened around the phone. He needed Wally if he wanted to start his new breeding program and would never manage to pay Clark's stud fee. Grace played a delicate role in this transaction, and he'd be damned if he'd let her screw it up. What good were daughters if not to create advantageous family ties?

'I'll talk to Grace. She might not make it down there for Christmas, but I'll bring her around.'

'Good. See that you do.'

Matt hung up. Lip curling, Edward dropped the phone in disgust and rubbed his hand over his stubbly chin.

What was he going to do about his daughter? He needed that bull and once they were family, he was sure he could use Matt's cross-breeding expertise to improve his herd and finally get White Peaks out of debt.

There were many advantages to selecting your in-laws and helping his children get the best out of life was one of them. He'd admit that Charlie could have done better. Zoe was a decent-looking girl and her mother gave them a discount at the bakery she owned, but that hardly kept their heads above water. The only reason Edward hadn't stopped the marriage was because Zoe's sister was married to Jason Taylor, which had given them the family connection to Tropic Sun. Not that a banana farm was any bloody good to them, but when they'd needed a grader last year, Jason Taylor had gladly handed his over to Charlie as that's what brothers-in-law did.

Now, Edward needed the same relationship with Redback. He'd taken the opportunity to introduce Grace and Matt at the rodeo, keen to see if they'd hit things off, but the kid had already been playing into Edward's hands and seducing Grace. Everything had been falling into place.

But while Grace had dallied at first, she hadn't fulfilled her role and now, the connection was slipping through Edward's fingers.

He downed the rest of his drink and slammed the glass onto the desk. Bloody woman. She would come around, whether she liked it or not.

* * *

Luke had no official training as a cook, but he knew food. He'd never worked in an actual kitchen, but he'd worked in many pubs and frequented even more cafés in his time. He'd also learned about nutrition once Joe had arrived in Elizadale and they'd become mates. Genuine nutrition based on science, not marketing to the public interest. Carbohydrates were his friend and vegetables filled every meal. Since dining out options were scarce, he usually cooked for himself and had become quite good at it too. He made delicious stir-fries and baked melt-in-your-mouth fish, both of which he'd include in his new menu. But he also had a taste for Mexican and a weakness for pasta, so he hoped to cater for a variety of cuisines.

But today's question was, what would he cook for Grace?

He was still pondering that as he pounded the treadmill on Sunday afternoon. Should he do the herb-encrusted salmon? She'd liked that idea on Friday, but he didn't have any fresh fillets. He had steak, but that was boring and then he remembered she didn't eat beef. So that only left chicken. He could do fajitas, but despite how much he liked those, he didn't plan to include them on the menu. It was a supply problem, as the kitchen couldn't possibly stock everything. Nachos would be enough to cover the Mexican element and everyone like nachos, but eating with their hands tonight didn't exactly spell a romantic evening.

Gritting his teeth, Luke straddled the treadmill and hit the stop button. Dammit, he wasn't looking for romance. He was simply having a woman over for dinner. It wasn't the first time.

But it was the first time he'd had Grace over, and while he could deny it all he wanted, he liked her.

'Just relax, idiot!' Running his hands through his hair, he headed for the shower. He had too many ideas and was keen to know what Grace thought about all of them. But there was one he wanted an answer to most of all, so after showering and dressing in a pair of denim shorts and a blue polo shirt, Luke entered the kitchen and grabbed the pineapple from the fridge. He'd do his coconut chicken, except instead of rice, he'd cook pineapple quinoa, since that's what he preferred. It was that touch fancier and, sue him, he wanted to impress Grace. So, he sliced up pineapple and onions, then began on the coconut sauce while trying not to let his imagination run wild.

But it was difficult. Luke wasn't sure what it was about Grace or why he'd taken more notice of her on Friday night. Yes, she was pretty, but he didn't need romantic complications right now, especially if she didn't feel the same way about him. She'd been chatty and keen to help him with the menu, but if her feelings didn't extend beyond that, he'd set himself up for embarrassment if he tried flirting with her.

So, he wouldn't. They'd be friends. They *were* friends in a younger-sister's-best-friend and known-you-all-my-life way. And that was enough.

But as a knock sounded on the door, every muscle in his body tensed. He took a deep breath as he abandoned his preparations and quickly washed his hands. Tonight was meant to be casual. She was just helping him out. Striding through the unit, he relaxed his shoulders and opened the door.

All the breath escaped his lungs and his hand tightened around the doorhandle.

Goddamn, she was beautiful. Her light brown hair flowed over her shoulders and she wore a well-fitted red top with cap sleeves that dipped low enough to show a hint of cleavage. Short denim shorts finished upper-thigh and red sandals adorned her feet.

Luke resisted a sigh. He was in trouble.

Chapter Seven

Grace had spent all day shoving thoughts of Luke from her mind, determined not to overthink the strange sensations that had been coursing through her veins since Friday night. He wanted her opinion on food, that was all. He may have stepped inside her personal space during that moment in his office and she may have wanted to kiss him, but that had been her foolish head talking.

Grace was done being a fool, so she ignored the butterflies in her belly and greeted Luke with a smile. 'Hey!'

'Hello.' He held open the screen door and let her in. 'Welcome. You look nice.'

Her step fumbled, although there was nothing but greeting in his compliment. 'Thank you. I like your place.'

She glanced around as he closed the door behind them to keep the air conditioning in. His duplex overlooked Abbott Street, the local name for the highway, and was a hop, skip, and jump away from Smithy's. The shared living and dining room filled the entrance while the kitchen was tucked around the corner behind the garage. His dark lounge looked plush and comfy, a worn rug decorated the floor, and a framed

North Queensland Cowboys memorabilia poster hung on the wall.

'Yeah, it'll do,' he said, slipping his hands into his pockets.

'And that's a massive TV.'

'Yeah, ninety-inch,' he said, and her eyebrows shot up. 'Hardly worth watching the footy on anything else.'

'Don't you have the projector at the pub?' she asked as he led her into the kitchen.

'Yeah, but sometimes I watch the game at home.'

And he loved his rugby league, even though she didn't know why anyone needed a TV that big. Especially in such a small lounge room.

'So, how was your day?'

Grace placed her bag on the kitchen bench. 'Good. Jess, Claire, and I went for a run this morning, did housework, then I went to work because a kid was sick. Inner ear infection and the little one wouldn't stop crying. I'm on call, but I'm sure we'll be fine.'

Considering the size of Elizadale, the doctor's surgery remained unattended outside of business hours, but Grace and Emma shared first on call and triaged patients. Most of the time, all people needed was reassurance, which Grace could sometimes do over the phone. But it was impossible to predict what would be on the other end of every phone call, and she needed to be ready for anything.

'That's all right. Hopefully, we won't be disturbed because I've got two courses planned. Dinner and dessert. I thought we would try the coconut chicken, but on pineapple quinoa instead of rice.'

Her mouth watered. She hadn't had quinoa since her uni days. 'How'd you get quinoa?'

Luke grinned as he took a bottle of Diet Coke from the

fridge. 'I used to stock up whenever I went to Mareeba, but I've recently convinced the supermarket to order it in for me. I promised Smithy's would buy it and the locals would catch on too, so if you like quinoa …'

Grace accepted the glass Luke handed her and smiled. 'Sure, I'll buy it. Quinoa's so good. I love it in salads.'

'Thanks. And yeah, it's my favourite wholegrain.'

Luke turned to his preparations and her belly rumbled. Dinner sounded delicious, but as her gaze trailed down his broad back, those warm sensations returned and flowed through her body. His blue shirt fit well, moulding to his chest and biceps before falling over the waistband of his knee-length denim shorts. Damn, the man was cut. Even his calves appeared to be made of steel and he had nice bare feet.

She sipped her drink. Would it be the worst thing to date her best friend's brother? If things worked out, she and Jessica could be sisters.

Grace gave herself a mental shake and leaned her hip against the kitchen bench. 'Dinner sounds good, Luke. Pineapple and coconut add a tropical flavour to the menu.'

'Exactly,' he said, mimicking her pose. 'I've suggested to Bill that we include tropical dishes and even some international cuisine since we're so close to Cairns and get a variety of tourists. Which is why I want stir-fry and spring rolls on the menu. I'm going to keep the banana split idea, but I don't want to do too much with bananas when that's the theme of Liam Maguire's café. Although what do you think of a chocolate fondue share plate?'

'Fondue? Could be romantic.'

He smiled softly. 'I thought so. It might draw people in for dates.'

Grace's hand tightened around her glass as Luke's gaze

held hers, his eyes as blue as the ocean off Port Douglas, except deeper and warm as they flickered across her face. Her pulse spiked.

'You could create that ambiance,' she breathed.

'Hmm ...' His body curved slightly. Towards her? The bench? She wasn't sure. 'Yes, I could. But maybe I should get cooking.'

He straightened and once he'd turned away, Grace blew out her breath. Then downed a mouthful of Coke.

'Do you need any help?'

'No, thanks. You just relax.'

Relax? How was she supposed to relax when her belly fluttered and heat ignited inside her chest?

'All right. So ... how was your day?' Ergh, lame.

'Same as you, I suppose,' he said, setting a skillet on the stove. 'Went for a morning run, then did the housework. I sometimes skip that, but I had you coming over, so there were no excuses.' He flashed her a smile over his shoulder and Grace gripped the countertop. 'Then I mowed the lawn, did my afternoon workout, and now we're here.'

Grace watched as he moved about the kitchen, placing a pot of quinoa on the stove while he waited for the skillet to heat. 'You work out a lot.'

'Yeah, but that's not news. I've always been an exercise junkie. Can't change that now.'

'I guess not. And there are worse things to enjoy. I was never into exercise until uni. I started jogging and then I fell in love with yoga. Did Jess tell you I want to open my own studio?'

Luke raised his eyebrows. 'No, but that's a great idea.'

Her spine relaxed at the change of subject. Talking about yoga was as calming as the practice itself. 'Thanks. I loved teaching in Mareeba and enjoyed driving there once a week since I could go shopping, but I wanted to do something that was all my own. And I think people in Elizadale would enjoy yoga.'

'It's empowering to have your own business, and I'm sure you'll find many people who will come to your class. I think Mum would. I wonder if Jess has mentioned it to her.'

'I'm not sure.'

'When are you going to open it?'

'Well, I can't open a studio right away, so I'm hiring the community centre for now and I have a "try-for-free" day booked on the sixteenth.'

'Of this month?'

'Yep. Just to get people interested, hopefully sell some multiclass passes as Christmas gifts, then I'll start regular classes in the New Year.'

Luke grabbed the chicken from the fridge. 'That sounds fantastic, Grace. Do you have flyers?'

'Yep. I'm distributing them tomorrow.'

'Well, feel free to bring some into the pub.'

She smiled softly. 'Thank you, Luke.'

'No worries, that's what community's all about. We need to help each other out. And I'm sure you'll get a steady group of regulars as yoga is quite popular.'

Raising her eyebrows, she sipped her drink. 'Have you tried it?'

'No,' he said, laying the chicken in the pan. 'And I have nothing against it, but I'm not sure yoga is my thing.'

'It isn't the same as weightlifting and not really what I call exercise. While yoga has physical benefits and can be intense, it's more about connecting with your body and mental wellbeing. But like I said, I have a try-for-free day.'

'And I wouldn't be very supportive if I didn't come to that.'

She swallowed a snigger. 'You don't need to.'

His gaze met hers, lines etching his forehead. 'Why wouldn't I?'

Blinking, she lowered her glass. 'You want to come?'

'Sure. Why not?'

Heart lurching, Grace couldn't suppress her grin. 'Luke, that would be amazing. I'd love to have you there. And bring your friends.'

Luke chuckled over the sound of sizzling chicken. 'If I'm going, I'll bully Joe into coming too. And if I manage that, he'll make the rest of the footy team come.'

Laughter erupted from Grace's belly as she imagined the Elizadale footy team with their butts in the air in downward dog. 'Oh my God, if you pulled that off, I'd kiss you.'

Luke stilled and Grace's spine stiffened. 'Shit, I'm sorry Luke.' Heat rose in her cheeks as she dropped her head into her hands. 'I didn't mean that. I just meant that I would be very grateful.'

The chicken spat in the pan. Luke cleared his throat. Grace peeked through her fingers as he turned and leaned on the bench opposite her, slipping his hands into his pockets.

'If that was the bet, Grace, I'd hardly need to convince the guys.'

She lowered her hands. 'What?'

'Just saying, if I told them I could win your gratitude by making them attend yoga, they'd all be there to tease and jeer. And if that's what it takes, then they come or I kick them off the team.'

Grace blinked again. The corner of Luke's strong mouth curled with amusement while his eyes …

Shit. Was that *interest?* Did Luke Smithfield *like* her?

Grace's cheeks flamed as she stepped backwards and glanced around aimlessly. 'I … I don't—'

In a few strides, Luke was in front of her. He reached for her shoulders but didn't touch her. 'I'm sorry. I didn't mean to upset you. It was a bad joke. I just—'

'But it wasn't a joke.' She met his gaze, chest constricting.

Luke exhaled. 'Maybe not entirely …'

Grace swallowed. She hadn't been expecting this. Luke wasn't supposed to like her. This evening was supposed to be friendly. Fun. She was there to help him. Not to … 'Did you invite me here because—'

'I invited you to dinner because I'm keen to get your opinion and your help with the menu,' he said before she could jump to any foolish conclusions. 'But I'll admit, the fact you were keen to help pleased me because … I do like you, Grace.'

Panic rose in her throat, but it didn't outweigh the swoon in her belly. Luke Smithfield, all six-foot bulging muscle of him, liked her. A man who had known her forever, who she'd played with in the pool as a kid. Her best friend's brother.

His bright eyes darkened as he took in the features of her face and heat descended into her thighs. It was the same look he'd given her on Friday night. And as her gaze dipped to his strong, masculine mouth, something deep inside her sparked.

Luke's hands dropped gently to her shoulders. 'I'm sorry I made a stupid joke,' he said. 'Especially if it made you uncomfortable.'

'No. Just took me by surprise. I never thought … you and I …' She shook her head. 'Sorry.'

'It's all right. If you want to just forget about it and stay for dinner, I'd be grateful. But if not—'

Her hands shot to his hips, brushing the edges of the denim. 'No. Luke, I—' Words caught in her throat. Usually she was much more articulate, but recent events had left her torn. She'd love to date and get to know someone on an intimate level, but what was the point? 'Of course I will stay. But I'd be lying if I said that I haven't been thinking about you since Friday night.'

His eyebrows quirked. 'Yeah?'

Her spine softened. 'Yeah. You looked good.'

'In my work clothes?'

'Yep. But I …' Shaking her head, she didn't know what she was thinking. He simply stared at her, his smile widening a fraction as his eyes glittered.

Then his hands ran from her shoulders down her bare arms and she stilled. Heat radiated along her skin. 'You shouldn't wear red.'

Her breath caught in her throat. 'What? Why?'

'Because …' His hands fell to her hips and a shiver coursed through her from head to toe. 'You look too damn sexy.'

Heat pulsed through her as her breath released in a whoosh. 'That might pose a problem,' she whispered, and his eyebrow quirked again. 'I wear a lot of red at Christmas.'

His strong shoulders slouched as his gaze fell to her red top. 'God help me.'

Grinning, she cupped his chin and lifted his gaze back to hers. 'Kiss me, Luke.'

He didn't need to be asked twice. Pressing his hand to the small of her back, his hot mouth captured hers and she stopped thinking. Lips pressed to lips for what felt like an eternity. Then his hand brushed up to caress the back of her neck and he eased her mouth open in a kiss that put her mediocre fantasies since Friday night to shame.

Grace sank against his body as she ran her hands down his torso, shivering at the sensation of hot, hard muscle beneath his cotton polo. He drew her lower lip into his mouth and she gasped as he plucked her off her feet and placed her on the bench. Inches apart, she caught his gaze. Yep, there was no mistaking it. Desire filled his deep, hooded eyes as he nipped gently at her lips. Grace moaned softly and ignored the prickling at the back of her neck. Luke slipped his fingers into her hair and she hooked hers through his belt loops, urging him a step closer as she returned his gentle but passionate kisses. Her pulse pounded. Breath caught.

A crackling sizzle sounded through the air, and Luke tore himself away. 'The chicken!'

Chapter Eight

As he leapt across the kitchen to lift the burning skillet off the stove, laughter rose in Grace's rasping throat. Then her mind caught up with her actions and the warmth around her heart curdled into a ball of doubt.

She bit down on her lower lip.

'Lucky save,' Luke said, placing the chicken back on the stove. Turning to her, his smile slipped. 'Grace?'

Her shoulders slouched and she dropped her chin to her chest. 'I'm sorry, Luke.'

'Hey. Look at me.' She had no other choice as he lifted her chin with a gentle finger. 'Why are you sorry?'

'I don't know what I was thinking.' This couldn't happen. Her father would hate it. He'd hurt her. Destroy Luke. 'I'm not in a good place right now and I shouldn't lead you on.'

His eyes clouded. 'Do you regret that kiss?'

'No.'

'Then what's the problem?'

Grace rubbed her hands against her thighs as a tightness formed in her chest. 'I don't know. I've made some terrible decisions lately.' Hiding her shame, she wouldn't tell him everything, but part of the truth came spilling out. 'I've had an awful week. And it's been a while since anyone cared about me. Or said they liked me or whatever.' Matt had said it, except that 'like' had only lasted for the night. 'But I'm sorry because I don't think I have anything to give. Relationship wise.'

'Right.' Nodding, Luke stepped back and scratched the back of his neck, his frown deepening and biceps bulging. He gestured towards the pot. 'I need to stir—'

'Go ahead.' She shooed him towards the stove, then gripped the benchtop and stared at the glossy tiles. Her heart ached. She didn't want to hurt him. She liked Luke and if there was any way they could date unscathed, she would happily try. But it was impossible. Her father knew everything that happened in Elizadale.

'But Grace …' Luke paused until she looked up and met his gaze. The smile he offered all but melted her into a puddle. 'I'd still love your help with the menu if you're happy to give it.'

Her shoulders slumped. 'I do want to help with that.'

'Good.' He leaned his hip against the stove as he stirred the pot. 'But I get where you're coming from. Relationships can be tough and it's been a while since I dated too.'

Grace nodded. She couldn't remember the last time Luke had had a girlfriend, not that she'd kept track and he was hardly the type to boast about such things.

'Dating rarely goes well for me,' she admitted softly.

'I haven't had much success either, but I don't like the idea of ignoring what's happening between us.'

Exhaling, she bit down on her lower lip. 'I know. I feel it too.'

'And we don't need to define it.' He switched off the stove

and set the pot aside. 'But that doesn't mean we can't explore it. I don't mind having "fun". But if you are strictly opposed to a relationship, tell me now and we'll lock this discussion away forever and stay friends.'

Grace's heart pounded against her ribs. She was out of her element. Was this what a mature, adult discussion felt like? Had she ever witnessed one?

She loosened her grip on the edge of the bench. 'I'm not strictly opposed.' Just terrified. 'Why? Are you looking for something serious?'

Luke shrugged. 'I'm an easy-going bloke, Grace.' His gaze left hers as he continued to manage the pots. 'But I will admit, I've always thought you're beautiful.'

Everything inside her tightened as she dropped her gaze again. She took a deep breath, but it didn't calm her. Why did her spine prickle? Why did this conversation feel awkward? Luke was being nothing but a gentleman and all she wanted was to run in the opposite direction. What was wrong with her?

Her stomach knotted. She knew what. But shoving that thought aside, she needed to say *something*, so Grace went with the first thing that came to mind. 'I'm hardly beautiful.'

Luke made a sound partway between a chuckle and a groan, and the tension eased. 'Believe what you want to. I think you are. So why don't we keep it casual?' He turned from the stove and slipped his hands into his pockets. 'Exclusive, but casual. If you're keen.'

Because he was. Luke didn't need to say it for Grace to see it in his eyes. And while the panic didn't subside, another part of her found comfort in his confidence.

'I'd like that,' she breathed. 'We can hang out, kiss and stuff, and I'll eat anything you want me to try on your menu.'

His mouth curved slowly, sexily, and Grace shivered. 'I'll keep you satisfied …' He moved towards her and placed his hand on her thigh. Grace's pulse skyrocketed. 'With lots of fresh, delicious food.'

She snorted out a laugh, and as he grinned, her body finally relaxed.

Luke's eyes sparkled as he pinched her knee. 'Sound good?'

'Yep.'

'Excellent. Because dinner's ready.'

Luke turned back to the stove and Grace slipped off the bench, breathing softly to get her pulse under control. She didn't want to worry or question what she'd got herself into. She shouldn't have to. It was her life and she would do what she wanted.

And what she wanted was to kiss Luke again.

Barely containing her smile, Grace gathered their glasses, the bottle of Diet Coke, and moved towards the table while Luke scooped pineapple quinoa into bowls. He laid the chicken on top and drizzled it with coconut sauce, then placed the aromatic meal in front of her as they sat opposite each other at the table.

'It looks wonderful, Luke.'

'Thanks. It might be simple, but coconut chicken is always a winner.'

'Sometimes that's what people want. Simple, delicious food.' But as she sampled her first bite, delicious was an understatement. The flavours exploded over her tongue, and she moaned softly. 'Wow, you really know how to cook.'

'Got to if you want to eat well.' He grinned around his fork. 'So, you like it?'

'Making it with rice will go better for the pub crowd, but yes. I love it.'

'Excellent.'

They ate a few mouthfuls in comfortable silence before he asked her about work, and she explained the running, drama, and unpredictability of smalltown medicine.

'Do you like that type of nursing in general practice?'

'Yeah.' She scooped more tiny balls of quinoa onto her fork. 'What I do here is a bit more than a general practice nurse would do in a city. Nursing is so varied and university placements exposed me to many types. But while I liked the procedural stuff and *loved* theatre, I enjoyed talking to people. Most of the time, I feel I'm outgoing.'

He nodded. 'I can see that.'

'So, I wanted to work with people. I almost did a graduate program at Cairns Hospital in paediatrics, but Joanne offered me a job here and I couldn't say no.'

'You like Elizadale.'

'I can't imagine living anywhere else.' Only on the rare occasion did she wish she'd taken the opportunity to escape the proximity to her parents, but Claire had opened her salon, Jessica had happily stayed in town working at the pub, and after three years living apart from them, all Grace had wanted was to come home. 'I love Elizadale Medical and working with Joanne and Emma. Plus, I get to fulfil different roles. I'm a general nurse and an emergency nurse. Not to mention a practice manager, phlebotomist, and X-ray technician.'

'Which makes you valuable to the community,' he said as they finished their dinner. 'Means we don't have to go into Mareeba as much.'

'Exactly.' If only her family could see that.

Luke stood to clear their plates, took them to the kitchen, then returned and offered her his hand. 'Come join me on the lounge.'

She didn't hesitate. Taking his hand, she moved with him to the lounge and sank into the chocolate-coloured cushions. Tucking her feet beneath her, she sat close enough to allow her shoulder to brush against his and caught a whiff of his soapy scent.

'Thank you for inviting me over, Luke.'

'Of course. I enjoy company.'

'Even nervous company?'

He arched his eyebrow. 'You were nervous?'

'Only before. I hadn't realised you felt that way about me. It took me by surprise and I wasn't sure what to think.'

Chuckling, Luke wrapped his arm around her shoulders and she sank further into his embrace. 'I never pegged you as someone who flustered easily. You were all confident and chirpy the other night in my office.'

'I guess I was just excited. About the menu. And I was keen to think about something other than the …' She stopped before she said 'fight with my parents'.

'Your bad day.' His hand brushed up and down her forearm. 'Do you want to talk about it?'

The fact he asked turned her insides to mush, but the last thing she wanted to do was talk about her father. 'It doesn't matter.'

'Okay …' His gaze darkened. 'Is there anything else you want to talk about?'

Grace swallowed. 'No. Why?'

'Because I'd like to kiss you again.'

Her shoulders softened and she grinned. 'I'd like to kiss you too.'

His mouth curved, then swooped down to hers. Grace cupped his face as Luke's arm snaked around her waist. She rose onto her knees and resisted the powerful urge to straddle him as she returned his kiss.

Luke's fingers brushed the small of her back, then snuck beneath her shirt to rest against her spine. Grace grinned against his lips. She could get used to this. Luke's mouth was warm, welcoming, and hinted at a touch of spice that made her ache for more. So much more. Dating might frighten her, but Luke could very well change her mind if—

A shrill cut through the air as the work phone rang.

* * *

Grace's groan vibrated through her throat and against his lips. 'Dammit, Luke. The phone.'

'Leave it.' She tasted so good. Hot, sweet, and fruity. He'd never intended kissing her tonight, but he wasn't complaining. Grace might have been nervous for reasons unclear, but her kisses were magic. Her body was spectacular. Toned and lean. Soft and sweet. Everything inside him heated and burned.

'No, I can't. It's the work phone.'

Luke stilled. 'Shit.'

'Yeah.'

Exhaling, he released her from his hold and glared at the unwelcome ringing as she hurried towards her bag. Her red T-shirt bunched halfway up her back, exposing the creamy skin that had been burning beneath his hands. Whether or not she believed it, she was damn cute. Beautiful, sexy, slender with just enough hip and pert breasts.

'Don't worry, they'll probably only need reassurance,' she called over her shoulder before answering the phone.

Luke sank into the lounge and ran his hands down his face,

ignoring the uncomfortable sensations her absence created. He wanted to remember where they were, wanted to continue to explore her body. Never in his wildest dreams had he imagined he'd be kissing Grace White on his couch, but he wanted this. He wanted to see where it would lead.

But as his heart rate slowed, so did his libido. He liked her, but he didn't want it to be like this. Getting hot and heavy on their first date wasn't like him because, yes, he would call it a date. He wanted to get to know her better. Romance her. So, as he caught her side of the conversation and the change in her tone, part of him was glad to realise that their evening was over.

'Okay, I'll see you there. Bye.' Grace hung up, her shoulders sinking as she returned to the lounge. 'I'm sorry.'

'Hey, it happens.' He stood. 'Someone's obviously unwell and needs you more than I do.'

'Thank you for understanding. I'm guessing severe dehydration secondary to gastro, so I'll need to go in to monitor and administer fluids. It's not worth the hassle for them to drive to Mareeba. But Luke ...' Her lips curved and dark eyes gleamed. 'I am disappointed we were interrupted.'

She inched closer and Luke's skin warmed. He reached for her hand and squeezed. 'Me too. I liked where this was leading. But we don't need to rush anything if you don't want to, Grace.'

He didn't know what had made her hesitate, but he didn't want to scare her away. He needed to do this right.

'I didn't mind where this was leading, Luke.' Her mouth curved. 'I do want to get to know you better. But ... I think we should keep things low key. For now.'

His brow furrowed. 'You mean ... secret?'

'No, I just don't want the rumour mill to whirl and ...'

Exhaling, she shook her head. 'We'll talk about this later. But I have to go.'

Heart hammering, Luke set her suggestion aside as he lifted her hand and kissed her small fingers. 'When are you off call?'

'Call changes over on Wednesdays.'

'Would you like to come over for dinner again?'

She smiled softly. 'I'd love to.'

A tightness formed in his chest. Wednesday seemed like forever away, but he was working the other nights and while he wanted her more than anything, he was a gentleman and he would wait. He didn't know what she was thinking, but she would never be a fling for him. So if she wanted to keep things quiet, fine. As long as it wasn't for long.

'I'll cook you something delicious then.'

'Sounds nice.' Grace drew her hand from his. 'And thank you for tonight.'

She grabbed her bag and slipped on her shoes. Luke followed her to the door, watching as she wriggled her fingers in a wave and slipped into her bright green hatchback. Once her taillights had disappeared, he let out a deep breath and ran his hands down his face.

His heart pounded. Blood rushed. He needed a good drink. Or a run.

Yeah, a quick jog on the treadmill to ease his frustrations, followed by a shower. A cold one.

Chapter Nine

Shane Campbell assisted his wife, Elanora, into a bed in the small ward. Elizadale Medical operated primarily as a general practice, but served other purposes given their rural location and had a small ward for emergencies to save locals the forty-minute trip to Mareeba. But even though the call-in had interrupted her hot evening, Grace was glad Shane had phoned. Elanora was terribly pale and weak, her mind foggy with exhaustion.

'When did the nausea and vomiting start, El?'

'This morning,' she whispered, barely able to keep her eyes open. 'It's worse now.'

'When I saw her this pale, I got worried.' Shane held his wife's hand on the other side of the bed while Grace wrapped a blood pressure cuff around her arm. 'She hasn't eaten or drunk anything since last night and now she can't stay awake.'

Grace pressed start on the monitor, then reached for the infra-red thermometer and held it to Elanora's white forehead. 'She's dehydrated. I'll take her vitals and call Joanne. I don't think she'll need to come in, but I'll hook El up to some fluids and monitor her closely.'

Elanora's breath escaped on a sigh. 'Thank you.'

Her high temperature didn't surprise Grace as she opened Elanora's chart on the computer and recorded her vitals. 'You'll be fine, El.'

She offered Elanora a reassuring smile, even though her patient's eyes were closed. Grace liked Elanora and had known her all her life. Elanora was a few years older than her, the eldest of the Kelly siblings, and the prep teacher at Elizadale State School.

Grace left the computer and returned to Elanora's side. 'Are you hot? Cold? Would you like the sheet on?'

She gave a small shake of her head. 'I'm good.'

'Okay. I'm going to run your status by Joanne, then we'll work on rehydration.'

Grace moved to the phone and explained the situation to the doctor.

'Give her a shot of Maxolon, administer IV fluids, and monitor her vitals. Call me back in an hour or if her temp goes up. I'll come by and see her then and hopefully she can go home.'

'Okay. Thanks, Joanne. Talk soon.'

Grace hung up and gathered what she needed. 'Okay, El, this'll make you feel better. I'm going to give you some Maxolon to help with the nausea. Just roll to your side for me.'

Grace administered the medicine into Elanora's glute, then inserted a cannula into her arm. She set the fluids up and within minutes, Elanora was feeling better.

'Maxolon's good stuff,' Grace agreed, repeating Elanora's blood pressure. It remained unchanged. 'You'll feel a lot better after some fluid.'

'Good.' Elanora's drooping eyelids opened as she lifted her gaze to Grace. 'I thought I was pregnant.'

Grace smiled gently and patted Elanora's knee. Everyone in town knew that Elanora was trying to have a baby. Grace supposed if she was thirty, had been married for four years and been with the man she loved since forever, she would want to have children too.

'It's all right. I'm sure this is just gastro or another bacterial infection, but you never know. Did you take a test?'

'I've run out, but it's too early in the month, so I can't be.'

Grace turned to the computer and made a note, even though she was sure Elanora was right.

For the next hour, Elanora remained stable. Her colour improved with the fluids and after Grace phoned Joanne again, the doctor came in. She examined Elanora's abdomen and put her diagnosis down to severe dehydration secondary to acute gastroenteritis, as Grace had suspected.

She set guidelines to discharge Elanora, then booked her an appointment for tomorrow.

'Call me if anything changes, Grace. Good work.'

After Joanne left, Grace took another round of vitals. Elanora's blood pressure had improved and her heart rate had reduced.

'I'm sorry, Grace.'

'What for?'

'You look great. Were you out?'

Grace glanced down at her simple outfit. 'I don't know about great, but yeah, I was at dinner.'

Elanora winced. 'I'm sorry.'

'It doesn't matter.' She smiled softly, meaning it. 'That's what I'm here for.'

She sent Elanora home looking a lot healthier with colour in her cheeks and a little steadier on her feet. Locking up the surgery, Grace's mind wandered back to Luke. The sensation of his lips on hers hadn't subsided as she'd worked. Nor had her embarrassment about her hesitation and nerves.

Groaning, Grace slid into her car. This was why she hated dating. What must he think of her? Was she sending mixed signals? She didn't want to. She hated holding back. Emma had been right on Friday night, and Grace didn't want to end up alone. Luke had a lot to offer. She enjoyed his company and conversation. He was kind and funny and she liked that he took care of himself. Plus, she wanted to watch a movie on his massive TV.

But once word reached her father …

Her stomach roiled as Grace pulled up outside Jackson Villas. She liked Luke. A lot. In an ideal world, they could date and have fun while eating magnificent food. Grace didn't want to deny herself the pleasure of spending time with him. Her father might want to control her, but she couldn't keep letting him hold her back. She would never please him, so why bother trying?

But while she longed to defy Edward, could she risk putting Luke in harm's way?

* * *

Grace spent the following morning in her usual Monday routine. She collected blood samples, completed a stock order, and followed up on Elanora Campbell. As she watched the fluid spread up the pregnancy test, Grace crossed her fingers, but only one line appeared. Sighing sadly, she slipped the negative test into the packet and took it to Joanne.

'I doubted it anyway,' Elanora said as Grace tightened the tourniquet around her arm. 'Like I said, it's too early. But we are trying and hopefully it'll happen for me this year.'

'I hope so too.' Grace palpated the vein, slipped the needle in, then attached the SST tube. 'But first, we better make sure you're healthy after last night's fun.'

Grace finished with Elanora and waved her goodbye. She set the blood tubes in the centrifuge to spin, cleaned until her samples were ready for collection, then found Emma to conduct a handover. Grace entered the staffroom and Emma's eyes lit up.

'How'd Friday night go?'

'What do you mean?'

'With Luke, silly!'

Grace aimed for casual, but failed to hide her smile. 'Like I said, I wanted to tell him what I thought of the lasagne.'

'*Aaa*nd?'

Emma's eyebrows quirked. Heart pounding, Grace bit down on her lower lip. Emma wouldn't spread gossip and Grace longed to tell someone. 'We had dinner last night.'

Emma clapped her hands together and grinned. 'I knew it! I'm so taking credit when this works out.'

Laughing, Grace collected her handbag from the locker. 'I'm taste testing his new menu. That's it.'

'Yeah right. And how does *he* taste?'

Grace's chest swelled. 'Pretty damn good.'

Emma almost danced on the spot. 'Oh, Grace, I'm so happy for you. Now, even though I'd love to talk about Luke all day, what do I need to know for this afternoon?'

Grace delivered her handover, then left the surgery. Checking her phone, she found five missed calls from her mother and her shoulders sank. Great. Francesca was bound to be fuming. As Grace started walking home, she called her mother back.

'Grace! Finally!'

'Hello to you too, Mum. What's up?'

'I hope you know your father's still not happy that you ended things with Matthew.'

'I'm sure he's not, even though there was nothing to end. Is that why you called?'

'No. Since you'll now be here for Christmas, I wanted to know what you'll bring for lunch.'

Yep, her mother sure knew how to make someone feel welcome. But what choice did she have? She might not like them, but they were her family and that's what Christmas was supposed to be about, spending time together.

'How about I make a dessert, salad, and whatever else you need?'

'Fine. And maybe some drinks? Charlie and Zoe are going to her family's place for the morning, but then they're coming here for lunch, so I want to have a big one.'

As if her father didn't have enough liquor already. 'I'll see what I can do. Let me know if you want me to make anything specific.'

'Okay. Are you going to Carols by Candlelight this weekend?'

'I'm going with Jess and Claire,' she said, emphasising her friends' names. Not that her mother noticed.

'Lovely! I'll see you there. I have to go now, Grace. Bye.'

Francesca was gone before Grace could reply. Slipping her phone into her pocket, she let herself into the unit, grateful Jessica and Claire were home and already had the air conditioner running.

'Hey!' Claire called as Grace dropped her bag by the door and fell into an armchair.

'Uh-oh.' Jessica frowned. 'What's wrong?'

'Family. I mean, seriously! Who needs them? Well, look

who I'm talking to. You two don't know how lucky you are. If you were dying, they'd all be at your side. Mine would probably have something else to do.'

Jessica reached across the space between them and took Grace's hand. 'Sweetie, your parents love you. Just in their own way.'

'Yeah ...' It would be nice to have a loving family like Jessica's to enjoy Christmas with, though. Her family were wonderful. Warm and welcoming. If she and Luke were to become more than casual ...

Grace quickly shook that thought away. She didn't need to add to her confusion there. Maggie uncurled herself from Claire's feet and, ever so loyal, wandered over to place her head on Grace's knees. The kelpie gave her 'don't worry about it' eyes and Grace smiled softly, rubbing Maggie's soft ears.

'Well, I have some news to lift your spirits!' Claire clapped her hands together, but Grace didn't tear her gaze from Maggie's. 'I was at book club last night and guess who's interested in your yoga class?'

'Who?'

'Sue and Heather.'

Grace's gaze shot up. 'Really?' Her friend nodded and, grinning, Grace rubbed Maggie's ears with extra enthusiasm. 'That is good news! If they become regulars, the whole town will come!'

Sue Riley and Heather Knowles were sisters who owned the local homewares store and were two of the most influential women in town. Sue especially since her husband Ron was a descendent of the town founder, Stuart Riley, and Elizadale's representative with the Mareeba Council. He owned many businesses and rental properties in town, including Jackson Villas, and was their 'Unofficial Mayor'.

Together, Sue and Heather overflowed with community spirit, headed many local committees, and regularly encouraged locals to follow their dreams with their unwavering support.

'Indeed,' Claire said. 'Heather asked why you hadn't done it earlier and Sue said she's keen to get stronger in her "old age".'

Jessica snorted. 'She's barely in her fifties!'

'Then I better have a shower and get my butt around to Elizadale Homewares.' Grace gently nudged Maggie aside and stood, excitement shimmying up her spine. 'Those flyers won't deliver themselves.'

Rushing upstairs, Grace quickly showered off work, changed, and grabbed the stack of flyers and business cards.

'Good luck!' her friends called as she waved and headed out the door.

Elizadale was a small town and, wanting the exercise, Grace left on foot. Sue and Heather had already been on her list, but knowing they were interested in yoga made it easier to walk into Elizadale Homewares. Their magnificent shop was filled with everything from tea-towels, quilts, and knitted items that Sue and Heather had made themselves to Rebecca Taylor's homemade candles, and various other handcrafted wares. Any local could approach the store to sell their work as long as they had a good business plan and quality stock.

'Grace! Just the woman I wanted to see.'

Grace smiled as a short blonde woman approached. 'Hi, Sue.'

'Claire told me about your new business venture.'

'Yes. I'm going to teach yoga at the community centre.'

Sue beamed. 'That's excellent! I've always wanted to try yoga. I mean, I stretch a bit and Joanne gave me direction to strengthen my pelvic floor once.' She leaned closer. 'It's never the same after having babies, you know. And I don't want to have troubles as I get older.'

Grace nodded, understanding completely. Working the pelvic floor was just as vital in yoga as anything else. 'Yoga can keep every part of you strong, Sue. Mind, body, and soul.'

'Then you can count me in. And Heather and Meg, of course.'

Sue's daughter Meg was another person Grace needed to talk to. Sue might be the influencer of her generation, but Meg Riley had inherited her parents' community spirit and was the golden girl in Grace's age group. If both Sue and Meg gathered their friends, she'd have enough people to deem the class a success. Not to mention Luke's joke about bringing the footy team.

Grace's heart filled. Yes. It was going to work out. 'I'd love it if you could all come. I have a try-for-free day Thursday next week and will begin classes in the New Year. Eventually, I want to open a studio.'

'Oh, yes. That could be viable. We don't have a lot of that sort of thing around here.'

They had no yoga, Pilates, gym, or fitness classes, just the local swimming pool and sports fields, but Grace wouldn't mention that.

'Thank you for thinking so, Sue. And as we progress, we can certainly work on things like the pelvic floor.' She could have many classes, including advanced, senior, and meditation only, but she wouldn't get ahead of herself. She would start with a basic yoga-for-everyone class once a week and grow it from there. 'Would it be okay if I left some flyers with you to display?'

'Of course! You know us, Grace. We're always happy to help.'

Smiling, Grace dug the flyers out of her bag. She'd doubted it would have been a problem since Elizadale Homewares had a dedicated display shelf to promote local events.

'Have you spoken to Vicki yet?'

Victoria Hall was the local baker, Sue's sister-in-law, and the mother of Grace's own sister-in-law, Zoe. 'Not yet, but I plan to stop by later.'

'She'll happily display one for you,' Sue said, setting Grace's flyers in a plastic stand by the register. 'Talk to Liam at the Tourist Centre too and put one up on the community notice board at the supermarket. Between those and your work, word will spread for sure.'

Grace hoped so. Thanking Sue, she skipped out of Elizadale Homewares and headed for the shopping complex on the corner of Riley Road and the highway. Vicki Hall had no problem taking a couple of flyers and Grace stuck one on the notice board at the supermarket too. Claire's salon was also in the complex, along with the butcher, a produce store, and hardware store, but she didn't bother talking to the owners of those. Hurrying across the road, she entered the Tourist Centre half concealed by scaffolding with the renovations for the café underway. It would be amazing once they opened, but for now, the place looked like any ordinary tourist stop with the abundance of brochures, commercial and local souvenirs, and the historic timeline that Jessica had painted on the wall. Liam Maguire wasn't there, but his casual staff member Isabella Brennan happily accepted the flyers, stating there would be no problem displaying them.

'I thought Mum mentioned something about this—' Isabella was Joanne's daughter and a few years younger than Grace '—but I wasn't sure when you were starting classes. I'll come along. I tried meditation once and found it very soothing. Yoga's meant to be good for anxiety.'

Grace nodded, understanding the cloud that passed through Isabella's eyes. 'I think you'll really enjoy it.'

The young woman smiled as she folded a flyer and tucked it into her pocket. 'I'll be there, Grace. Thank you.'

Considering that a job well done, Grace danced her way home. She remained on a high as she worked steadily through Tuesday and spent an hour after dinner texting Luke. He was at work too, but apparently not very busy. And since he didn't have a boss to reprimand him, he saw no reason not to text while on the job. They discussed normal things mostly, then the conversation simmered as he replied, **I can taste your lips … your skin. I can't wait to hold you again.**

Warmth rushed over her, and Grace grinned like a loon. She'd forgotten how exciting it was to flirt and tease. She wanted to be in his arms too, to run her hands over every nook and cranny of him and get a peek beneath his shirt.

Her fingers shook as she replied. **Me too …**

Chapter Ten

Somehow, Grace made it through Wednesday and returned from work with heat in her heart and jiggles in her belly. Showering, she shaved her legs and applied shea body yoghurt to her skin. Not that she planned to take things all the way since it was only their second 'date', but it never hurt to be prepared. So, she slipped on her best underwear, then tore the tag off her new red dress. Zipping it up the side, she straightened the clingy material over her hips and breasts, then grinned at herself in the mirror.

Yeah, perhaps she was sending a certain message. She looked bloody hot. Was it too much?

Her father's cruel words seeped through her conscience. *Give a bloke the wrong idea … What do you expect if you tease them … Dammit, show a bit of leg, girl.*

Shuddering, Grace closed her eyes. No. She could wear what she wanted. Have a bit of fun. Her father was wrong. She'd known that for years.

Grace pressed her hand to her belly and let out a deep breath. With her thoughts under control, confidence shivered along her skin again as she buckled up her glittery sandals. She liked Luke, wanted to look nice, and dammit, she wasn't backing out.

All she needed now was to get past her friend. Grace arrived downstairs and Claire glanced up from the lounge.

She frowned. 'Where are you going in that dress? I thought you were keeping that one for a special occasion?'

Grace shot her a smile. 'All nights are special occasions. I'm just … going out.'

Claire's eyebrows shot up. 'On a date?'

'I'm not …' Except Grace couldn't lie to her best friend. Torn, she grabbed the door handle and shrugged. She wanted to tell her friends—eventually—but she couldn't tell Claire about Luke before she told Jessica. 'I'm just going out.'

'I'll find out!' Claire called after her. 'You can't keep secrets from me!'

'Goodnight, Claire!' Grace stepped outside into the heat and pulled the door closed behind her. She slipped into her car, drove down Stuart Road, and turned onto Abbott Street. The sun set behind the tree-lined creek and the rosy tulip trees that lined the highway cast shadows over the bitumen.

Her pulse quickened as she parked behind Luke's sleek red Holden Commodore ute. Dropping her hands from the wheel, Grace took a deep breath and let it out slowly. Nerves prickled her skin. But after another few breaths, the pranayama eased her tension. Screw her fears. She wanted this. She wanted to enjoy life, be young, take control, and have fun. Any repercussions were problems for another day.

Steeling her spine, she stepped out of the car and adjusted her dress. Grace relaxed her shoulders and knocked. Seconds later, the door opened and Luke pushed back the screen.

His face hardened like granite. 'Dammit, Grace. I told you not to wear red.'

Grinning, she stepped towards him and caught a whiff of his delicious, soapy scent. His hair was still wet from his shower and the workout he'd undoubtedly done earlier radiated heat from his body.

'Oh, Luke.' She placed her hand on his shoulder, only an inch of sizzling summer air separating them. 'You seriously didn't think I'd wear anything else, did you?'

He stared at her for an eternity, blocking the air conditioning. After a few drumming heartbeats, he muttered, 'Dammit,' and swooped down to capture her grin with his mouth.

Grace giggled as his hands hardened on her back. Wrapping her arms around his neck, she opened herself up for more and Luke dived into her, nipping hungrily at her lips.

Yes, she could get used to this. But before she lost herself completely, Luke drew away and stepped back. 'Come in, Grace.'

Knees shaking, she stepped inside, welcoming the ambient temperature drop of ten degrees. If only the same could be said for the heat curling inside her belly. She took a deep breath and smiled at the scent drifting from the kitchen. Garlic? Herbs? 'Something smells good.'

'I thought we'd try the herb-encrusted salmon,' he said, striding towards the kitchen. Grace kicked her sandals off at the door, dropped her bag, and followed him.

'Yum. I'll admit, fish is my favourite meat.'

'Mine too. Salmon, mackerel, and barramundi. Can't get much better than that.' He reached for a prepared tray of potatoes and slipped them into the oven. 'Now, let me get you a drink. Do you drink anything other than Diet Coke?' he asked, opening the fridge.

'Sure, as long as it's not full of sugar.'

'Do you like coffee?'

She nodded as he poured them both a drink. 'I don't mind coffee. Jess, Claire, and I enjoy visiting the coffee farms around the Tablelands.'

'Jacques Coffee is pretty good, and I like their food.'

'Jacques is nice, and so's Skybury. The Kellys need to do something like that and open their own coffee house. Or at least have a gift shop where you can buy their beans.'

'It wouldn't be the worst idea,' Luke agreed, opening the freezer. 'They grow fine beans, and I believe Liam's using their coffee when he opens the café.'

'That'll be something, at least. I'm looking forward to that opening as it'll be nice to have a place to go for lunch or coffee dates.'

Luke smiled from where he was preparing vegetables. 'Perhaps we can have a coffee date.'

Grace's hand tightened around her glass, warmth radiating through her. She'd love nothing more. They could sit on the patio overlooking the parkland and sip coffee on a cool winter's morning, perhaps after finishing a jog together. But that would mean they would be seen as a couple. Even if they said they were 'just friends', gossip would spread like wildfire. Secrets couldn't be kept in a small town and if people started talking …

Grace's heart pounded. 'That sounds nice, Luke. But … well …'

'Then we'll have to tell people. Which you don't want to do.'

There was no mistaking the hint of bitterness in his tone. Exhaling, Grace ran her fingers through her loose hair. 'It's not that I don't want to, but people can be so nosey. Plus, I don't want Jess finding out that we're seeing each other and then getting upset that I didn't tell her. So, I'm thinking I should be the one to do so.'

Luke's shoulders softened and the tension eased from Grace's body as he nodded. 'If you like. I don't think she'll mind though.'

'No, I don't either. We might find it awkward at first as girlfriends usually talk about that stuff, but that changes when it involves someone's brother.'

Luke's mouth curved as he fixed lids onto the microwave dishes. 'That's a relief. She'll probably just tease you about having no taste. Isn't that what sisters think of girls who date their brothers?'

That's what Grace had once thought of Zoe. 'I guess. She'll shake her head and ask what I see in you.'

He quirked his eyebrow. 'And do you see something you like?'

Grinning, she placed her glass on the bench and moved towards him, holding his gaze as she touched her finger to his hard chest and slowly traced the length of his sternum. His eyes darkened. 'I think I do …'

'Good.' Voice husky, he swooped down and pressed his hot mouth to hers, caressing her hip and urging her closer. Fire shot through her veins. But as quickly as he'd kissed her, he drew away and stepped back. 'But I don't think you have much to worry about, Grace. Jess is easy going. Brothers are more likely to get overprotective.'

Catching her breath, she swallowed a snort. Grace didn't know much about overprotective big brothers. She could have men use her every which way her father wanted them to, and Charlie wouldn't give a shit.

'If you say so,' she replied as he placed enough space between them to simmer the heat. 'But anyway, I want to be the one to tell Jess that we're … doing whatever it is we're doing.'

'How about we just call it dating?' Luke suggested, slipping his hands into his pockets. 'I know I said we didn't need to define it, but dating doesn't sound too scary, does it?'

The warmth in his eyes softened her spine. He was right. She might have been nervous at first, but if she continued to come for dinner and kiss him, then dating covered it.

'Okay. We're dating. But I want to wait to tell Jess. I don't need her pestering me for details.'

'Fair enough.' He strode towards the fridge. 'I won't say anything to her and you let me know when you do.'

'Thank you.'

But the agreement did nothing to settle her anxiety. Eventually, her father would find out and the sabotage would begin. She didn't want him to hurt Luke. He might be tough and unlikely to succumb to her father's manipulation, but Grace couldn't risk it. She needed to protect him.

Luke refilled her glass, then placed the bottle aside and wrapped his arms around her waist. 'I'll leave it in your hands, but just so you know, I'd be proud to tell people I'm seeing you, Grace. You're a kind, beautiful woman, and my mother would be delighted to hear that I'm dating you.'

Thankfully he was holding her upright because she all but melted as his fingers brushed the base of her spine.

'But I know that you have a rocky relationship with your family,' he continued softly, and a lump rose in Grace's throat. 'A bloke hears things, Grace. So, if you don't want to tell them, then that's fine.'

She stared at him. It was no secret that her relationship with her family was strained, but had he been reading her mind? What kind of gossip had he heard? Probably a lot over the bar. Many of her father's acquaintances and workers frequented Smithy's. They could have recounted many stories or vented their frustrations over a beer.

'It's not just that,' she said. 'I mean, yes, I don't think my family would welcome you as yours would me.' Hell, Mary and Nick Smithfield already claimed her as a daughter, being Jessica's best friend and all. She'd spent many nights sleeping over, playing in their yard, and enjoying Mary's delicious buckwheat pancakes for breakfast. 'But … I do like you, Luke. And I don't want any opinions from my family infecting our little bubble.'

He chuckled, swooped in for another kiss, then stepped away. 'If you think that's best. Now, I better put the salmon in else we'll never eat.'

Luke took the salmon he'd already prepared from the fridge and slipped it into the oven. Thankfully, he dropped the subject of her family and asked, 'Did you do well with your flyers?'

'Yes! Everyone were happy to take some, and I have generated a lot of interest. More people responded to my free class on Facebook too.'

'Awesome. I told Joe we had to go. He looked at me like I was nuts, but he agreed because he likes supporting others.'

Grace pressed her lips together. The image of Joe, who was taller and broader than Luke, stretching out at yoga was even more amusing. 'Thanks.'

'And I was right about Mum too. She's keen to try it. But I need to know, how does a yoga class work?'

'Everyone teaches differently, but I like to start with breathing exercises, then work on core while everyone's lying on the floor,' she said. 'Then we stand for strength poses, do a bit of lunge work with twists, and then stretch before savasana.'

His eyebrows quirked. 'Savasana?'

'Relaxation.'

'Is that where you lie on the floor and do nothing?'

'It's not nothing. You stop thinking and relax. Yoga's more about connecting and being in tune with your body than anything else. And it feels good to lie still after putting your body through all that strengthening and stretching.'

'I suppose.' He shrugged his broad shoulders before setting the vegetables in the microwave. 'I'll still give it a go.'

'You'll enjoy it for what it is. If not, I'll appreciate you coming anyway.'

'And I appreciate you testing my menu.'

She laughed. 'Trust me, it's my pleasure.'

Grace might not have considered herself a foodie, but she'd never had more fun talking food and menus with Luke. And how could a girl complain about having a handsome man cook for her? Especially when she soon found herself seated with another delicious meal to enjoy. The square of salmon with a crispy herb crust was perfectly portioned, the spiced potato wedges had her mouth watering, and the steamed vegetables of carrot, beans, and cauliflower added colour to the plate.

Everything was delicious.

'When do you think you'll launch the new menu?'

'I need to get Bill to agree by next week, then we should be ready to launch on New Year's Eve.'

Grace's eyebrows shot up. 'So soon?'

He shrugged and sliced into his fish. 'It might help draw

the crowd and be a great way to welcome in the New Year. And I think we can pull it off that quickly in our little town.'

'Probably. And that's great, because I'm telling you, I'd pay to eat this at Smithy's.'

Luke grinned. 'You won't have to pay to eat it here.'

'Ooh, enticing.' She crossed her ankles and squeezed her knees together. 'Will it come with dessert?'

'It comes with dessert tonight. What do you think about apple crumble?'

'I love apple crumble. Fruity desserts are my favourite.'

'They're good. Especially with chocolate. I'll have to make you some choc-raspberry mousse.'

'Oh, stop. Now you're teasing me.'

'Well, I *had* made the mousse on Sunday, but we were interrupted.'

She frowned. 'Then why aren't we having it tonight?'

'I ate it. Including yours. But tonight ...' He took her hand and squeezed. 'There will be no interruptions.'

Grace's pulse quickened as she hastily swallowed a carrot. 'No.'

She'd never been more grateful for anything. The sizzling attraction between them set her skin on fire and after the money she'd spent on this dress, it deserved to have Luke peel it from her body. It was Christmas and she should treat herself. And right now, all Grace wanted was Luke.

They finished dinner and Grace took their plates to the sink.

'Would you like dessert now?' Luke asked, following with their glasses.

'No, thanks. I think we should let dinner settle first.' Turning from the sink, she wrapped her arms around his waist and pressed her hands over the hard planes of his back. Imaging how much weight he rowed to build such muscle, she shivered and met his spectacular blue eyes.

Luke reached up and twirled a lock of her hair around his finger. 'Did you want to watch a movie?'

As much as she wanted to discover the attraction of his massive TV, Grace shook her head. 'But we could return to the lounge and pick up where we left off on Sunday?'

He quirked his eyebrow, brushing his fingers through her hair to caress her neck. She melted into his touch. 'Oh, yeah?'

Throat tightening, she nodded. 'I was ready to take your shirt off when that damn phone rang.'

He grinned. 'You want to take my shirt off?'

Grace ran her hands around his ribs and up his chest to rest on his shoulders, delight joining the heat simmering in her veins. 'Is that an invitation?'

Eyes softening, Luke's hand dropped from her neck and brushed down the side of her body, leaving shivers in their wake. 'If you do, I might want to return the favour.'

Her knees buckled. She didn't want to think. Didn't want to hesitate. Grace's spine steeled. She was in control and dammit, she wanted to fulfil the desires that had been simmering since Friday night.

Smiling softly, she rose onto her toes and stopped a breath from his parted lips with her gaze on his. 'My zipper is on the side.' Then she kissed him.

Luke pulled her close, his strong arms holding her in a warm, welcoming vice as his tongue plundered. Every nerve ending responded as her blood heated and her thighs burned. Luke's fingers dug into her hips until he possessed her and soft moans escaped her throat.

Gripping the hem of his shirt, Grace slipped it up his hard

body. It stuck. Luke drew away, grabbed his collar, and lifted it over his head.

Grace's breath escaped as her hands fell to his abs. Shit, all eight of them were present and on display, rippling hot beneath her fingers.

'Do you approve?'

'Oh, yeah.'

His eyes blazed. 'Your turn?'

'Yes, please.'

She lifted her arm to expose her zipper and held his gaze, her heart pounding hard and slow as he tugged it down. Her dress loosened, exposed her hip, and she lowered the straps. It took a bit of shimmying, but the dress pooled at her feet and Luke's hands fell to her waist.

'Wow.'

She grinned. 'Do you approve?'

Chuckling, Luke pulled her close. 'You're beautiful, Grace. Every part of you. But damn, you're hot.'

The sizzle inside her deepened. 'Let's forget about the couch. I think we can have more fun in the bedroom.'

'All righty, then.' Scooping his hands beneath her, he hoisted her up. Grace yelped but had just enough time to wrap her legs around his hips as he carted her out of the kitchen. 'Dessert will keep.'

They entered his room and Luke knelt on the bed, lowering her gently before switching on the bedside lamp. Grace's breath caught as her hands splayed over his magnificent pecs. She wanted to taste every nook and cranny of him, and she would, but as Luke lowered his head to kiss the sensitive flesh between her breasts, Grace let him explore first. His hand snuck beneath her back and she arched. Her bra clasp loosened and she freed herself.

Luke's mouth captured her breast and she melted into the mattress, gasping as his tongue circled the sensitive peak. Her hands gripped his hair, holding him against her as he moved to provide her other breast with the same attention.

'You taste divine.'

Grace grinned as she closed her eyes, enjoying the sensations pulsating through her. With the weight of his body over hers, she longed to take the time to soak him in. He was hard, the lot of him. Hard, perfectly sculpted muscles. She ran her hands down his shoulders, shivering at the ripples and contractions beneath her fingers.

Luke moved lower, his lips trailing down her belly as his hands caressed her sides. Grace brushed her fingers through his hair before letting her arms fall back over her head, arching her body against his mouth. Pleasure took hold, fire raging along her skin and pooling in the ache between her legs. Then he stilled, his breath hot against the waistband of her pink lace knickers. His fingers hooked in around her hips. Grace bit down on her lower lip, aching for him to continue. To touch, taste, or kiss her. But he retreated and her eyes flew open, meeting his gaze as he slid back up her body and took her hand in his.

Her heart lurched. Had he changed his mind? *No!*

Then his mouth curved. 'You ready?' he asked, his voice gravelly.

Her breath escaped in a whoosh. 'Oh, God, yes.'

She gasped as he cupped her, slipping his fingers beneath her knickers. Grace ignited.

'You are ready …'

This was bloody torture, but in the best way. 'I want nothing else. Thought of nothing else. Dammit, Luke …'

She reached for the clasp of his shorts and flipped them

open. Thankfully, he took the hint to hurry and removed his hand from her. Rolling away, he kicked the denim off while Grace slipped her knickers down her legs, removing all the remaining barriers. Luke reached into the bedside drawer for a condom, and everything inside her tightened as she watched him slip it on and turn back to her.

She sank into the mattress as he positioned himself on his elbows. Grace wrapped her arms around his shoulders and pulled him closer until his hard chest lay over hers. Lifting her leg, she ran her foot over his taut calf, her toes curling in anticipation as she held his wanton gaze. Then his arm looped beneath her knee, lifting her hip as he slid inside her.

She cried out softly, gasping as he moved deeper. His name escaped on a whisper as his fingers dug into her thigh. Grace let herself go, slipping into another world that only he could take her to. Her nails clawed at his shoulders as they rocked, heat building inside her until she climaxed in a burst of shattering stars.

Already? Damn ... They weren't even done. Far from it. Grace wanted more. Wanted this feeling to last forever as she opened her eyes to meet his.

Luke's mouth came down over hers, swallowing her next gasp. She sucked on his lower lip and then his tongue plundered. Her other leg wrapped around his hips to bring him deeper. She needed him to fill her. Needed to build. He grew hotter and larger, preparing for his own climax, but she wanted to beat him to it or at least meet him at the finish.

They broke their kiss, needing to breathe. He found the right spot and she clenched around him, moaning through her second orgasm as he found his own. Grace cried out as Luke's fingers squeezed her thigh.

Then they stilled, gasping for breath. Her arms slackened

around his shoulders and he released her leg. Grace welcomed the sensation of Luke collapsing over her.

* * *

They didn't move for several minutes. Tangled together and chests heaving, Luke's heart threatened to explode as he tried to catch his breath.

Eventually, he swore softly into the pillow. 'That was amazing.'

Grace laughed and ran her hand down his back. 'I know. Damn, Luke. I don't think I want dessert.'

'We'll need to eat. Or at least I will.' He lifted his head and grinned, warmth filling his chest. 'Though I'm not sure the apple crumble will do much for carb loading. I'm going to need the energy. That's if you want to do it again.'

'There are enough carbs in the apple crumble, I'm sure. And we better eat it because that's never going to be something we only do once.'

Staring into her eyes, he stilled. 'You were great.'

'Ha! You were.'

'No, really.' Luke lifted himself onto his elbows. He knew he shouldn't say it, but he couldn't hold it in. 'I'm thinking … Grace, this dating thing might work out.'

She tore her gaze from his flexed biceps, her eyebrows shooting up. 'What do you mean?'

He noticed her alarm. Her surprise. But it didn't bother him. He could work with her fear of relationships. He was in no hurry and could relate. The warmth, longing, and desire he felt for her were scary as hell. But nothing would stop Luke from embracing it.

What was stopping her?

Swallowing, he brushed his fingers across her delicate cheek. 'I like you. I want to get to know you better. And to have you in my bed as often as possible.'

Her mouth curved a little, but her eyes glistened more. 'Well ... I like you too. And if that's the case, then *I* should get to know *you*.'

Her legs tightened around his hips and arms wrapped around his shoulders, pushing against him. It took a moment for Luke to realise what she wanted, so he relaxed and let her roll him onto his back.

'Next time,' she said, 'you're going to be under me.'

'I won't argue with that. But first, we should fix ourselves up here.'

She climbed off him as he sat up to remove the condom. Then she placed her hand on his shoulder and urged him back against the pillows before throwing her slender thigh over his legs. Her hands fell to his pounding chest as her gaze soaked in his body. Heat flowed through him at her appraisal. He didn't boast about it, but he put in a shitload of effort into his body and was proud of how he looked.

'The workouts do you good ...' Spreading her fingers over his pecs, she lowered her head of glorious caramel waves and kissed his sternum. His breath shuddered from his throat.

'That's the point.'

'Hmm ...' Shivers coursed through his belly as she ran her hands down the groves and bumps of his abs. 'I loved studying anatomy at university.'

'Is that so?'

'Ahuh. I didn't learn as much about muscles as we did other things, but it gave me a deeper appreciation for the human body. You'd be magnificent to learn on with all of your perfectly defined muscles.'

He brushed her hair over her shoulders before trailing his fingers over her creamy collarbones. 'You're beautiful too, Grace.' He took in the swell of her breasts, her narrow waist, and taut thighs. 'Yoga undoubtedly does you good.'

'It keeps me toned well enough. We should work out together one day.'

'Which way? Weights or yoga?'

'Whatever you like. I enjoy gym work. Or we can go jogging.'

'Hmm … one day.' He gripped her hips and felt the quiver of her belly beneath his thumbs. 'But right now, I prefer we do this.'

'Me too.'

She kissed him, and Luke drew her wicked tongue into his mouth. Letting himself go, he drowned in her taste, her touch, the way her skin felt beneath his hands as he caressed her bottom.

For the rest of the night, Luke lost himself in Grace.

Chapter Eleven

Grace spent the following couple of days in a daze as doubt and delight wreaked havoc upon her mind. She couldn't get Luke's confession out of her head. He liked her. Wanted her. She couldn't dispute that, as not only had he told her, he'd also shown her. And she longed to embrace it. Luke possessed many qualities that she liked in a man. He was kind and funny, so they could easily get along. He was a fabulous cook and they felt the same way about food. Luke also wasn't afraid to say it like it was, so there were no communication problems. And he cared about his family, something she couldn't help but feel envious of. Because his family cared about him too.

And she wanted that more than anything.

Sighing, she mixed the ice in her Diet Coke as she sat at the Smithfield Hotel on Friday afternoon watching her friend tend the bar. That was another thing. She needed to tell Jessica sooner rather than later. Grace didn't want to keep her new, fun, and exciting romance with Luke to herself and telling her friends was at the tip of her tongue. But she couldn't find the words, so Grace said nothing of it and chatted happily with her friend. Apparently, Luke was in the office doing bookwork and was taking forever to emerge and join them at the bar.

'Last day of school today,' Jessica said as she filled a cup of straws. 'The teachers are having their Christmas party tonight.'

'That'll keep you busy.'

'Should do. And Tiffany's leaving, so we'll be getting a new teacher for the grade ones.'

'It's nice having new people in town. Even nicer when they stay.' Professionals regularly blew through Elizadale, using their small town to gain experience before returning to the city. 'And you never know, we might get a new doctor next year too.'

'Hmm … maybe a young and cute male doctor?'

Grace laughed. 'What does it matter to you? You have Cade.'

'Not yet, I don't.' Jessica's gaze strayed behind Grace's shoulder. 'And speak of the handsome devil …'

Grace turned, withholding a grin at the sight of super sexy Cade Wilson. Tall and lean with the most handsome face known to mankind, he'd always been drool-worthy with his dark hair, amazing dark eyes, and a grin that even made Grace swoon.

Accompanying him today was none other than his equally sexy best friend Adam Maguire. Seeing him at the Smithfield Hotel only ever meant one thing.

'Georgina kick you out again, Adam?' Jessica asked as the men approached.

Grace stifled a laugh. With the pale bruise around Adam's left eye, he'd undoubtedly been in another brawl with one of the Kelly brothers and, therefore, the feisty owner of the Royal Hotel had kicked him out again.

Adam flashed his charming bad boy grin and slid onto the

stool beside Grace. 'Is that the only reason you think I visit you, Jess?'

'Seems that it is. You two want a beer?'

'Thanks.' Adam turned to Grace, his grin widening. 'Hey, Gracie. How's it going?'

She'd given up years ago trying to stop him from calling her Gracie. Adam did what he wanted, not that she minded the nickname. He might be her ex-boyfriend, but she still liked Adam as a person. Even though he found himself in trouble at times, he was a decent bloke with an irresistible charm that eventually won people over.

'I'm all right,' she replied. 'What'd you do to piss off Paul and Harry?'

'What does he always do?' Cade asked. 'Jordan.'

Adam sighed and leaned his forearms on the bar. 'That was not the problem.'

'No, dumping her was.'

'Why do you even go out with her?' Jessica asked, placing Great Northerns in front of the men.

'You don't "go out" with Jordan.' Adam actually used air quotes. 'Besides, she's the one who dumped me and moved onto some other bloke, which was what I tried to tell Paul. But he's been in a downright terrible mood these past few months. I think he's making a habit of punching me every few weeks.'

Grace sipped her drink to hide her smile. She didn't want to be amused, but some things never got old. Although why Adam put up with Jordan, Grace would never know. She hadn't liked Jordan since the woman had spread lies about her and tried to steal Adam away, thankfully to no avail.

'Paul will grow up one day. Surely it happens to everyone.' Hopefully, it would happen to Adam if a miracle woman ever passed through town. 'So, you're going to drink here for the next week? Is that all your sentence is again?'

'Yeah. May as well keep Cade company.'

'Luke will be thrilled,' Jessica commented dryly. 'Don't cause fights here though, else he'll kick you out too.'

Adam snorted. 'Luke hasn't kicked me out in years.'

Grace smiled. Just thinking about Luke brought a pleasurable burn to her thighs, which wasn't something she needed when hours remained until she could do something about it. So instead, she focused on the conversation as Jessica asked Cade about his day.

'Picked up quite a few people for speeding. One was doing twenty kilometres over the limit.' Cade shook his head. Ever since he'd returned to Elizadale as a police officer, he'd become a highway fiend and every local knew to watch their speed as Cade spent half his week out on patrol. Not that Grace could blame him as speeding continued to be a problem and there had been enough accidents on the roads.

Then her skin prickled, and a strange warmth settled over her as Luke's deep voice shivered up her spine.

'So, is Kelly at home nursing a broken nose?'

Luke stepped behind the bar, irritation flashing through his eyes at the sight of Adam in his pub. Grace grinned in his direction. Damn, he looked good. He only wore his regular Smithfield Hotel polo and jeans, but remembering the way his body had rippled a harmony beneath hers had her toes curling around the footrest of the barstool.

'I wish,' Adam replied with equal disinterest, nudging Cade. 'This one pulled me off him before I had the chance. But don't worry, Smithfield. I won't cause trouble.'

'You better not.'

Then, without another word, Luke slipped into the cold room and closed the door behind him. Grace blinked. What was that? He hadn't even looked at her. Or smiled. What about a 'Hey, Grace'? Sure, they'd agreed to keep their relationship quiet, but to not even acknowledge her?

Her shoulders slumped. No, it wasn't a big deal. He was at work. Busy. It was fine. There was no need to overthink things. Luke would come and say hi when he had a spare moment.

'Are you two going to the carols tomorrow night?' Jessica asked, and Cade nodded.

'Yeah, I'll be there with the family.'

'Me too,' Adam said, taking a swig of his beer. 'Can't miss an opportunity to hear Meg sing.'

Indeed. Meg Riley was a talented singer whose musical dreams had never come true, but Grace loved watching her at the Christmas carols, which was one of the few occasions she performed.

'Is Jack going too?' she asked, and Adam shrugged.

'Wouldn't matter. That brother of mine has bloody rocks in his head. He'll lose Meg if he doesn't make a move.'

Grace laughed. 'I doubt that. Some things are just meant to be.'

Adam scoffed. 'You're entirely too romantic, Gracie.'

'Ha! Just you wait. One day, you'll fall in love, Adam Maguire, and you won't have the first idea what to do about it.'

'I don't shy away from a challenge. If the right woman showed up, I wouldn't muck around. And I certainly wouldn't keep her waiting years.'

Grace smiled around her straw, distracted by the ridiculous notion of Adam ever falling in love.

Her phone vibrated and, reaching into her bag, Grace pulled it out. She glanced at the screen and stilled.

It was Matt Clark.

Heart pounding, she excused herself and hurried across the pub. Why was he calling her? Hadn't she made herself clear? He certainly had after their night at the rodeo by chatting up that other girl. But he'd called her a few times lately and the last thing she needed was him to continue his pursual of her when he settled on Redback in the New Year.

Stepping outside, she pressed the green button. 'Hello.'

'Hey, Grace. Surprised you answered.'

Leaning back against the pub's rendered wall, she exhaled and crossed her free arm over her chest. 'You'd only have kept calling.' She'd already learned that lesson.

'Probably,' he mused as though seeing nothing wrong with that. 'I just wanted to talk to you. See if you've changed your mind about my offer.'

Grace's arm tightened around herself as she stared across the highway towards the parkland. 'I don't think so, Matt.'

Annoyance radiated off his deep exhale. 'Then I thought I'd let you know I'd be up there earlier than planned. By New Year. Thought maybe we could head to Port Douglas. Have ourselves a party.'

Gritting her teeth, Grace stepped away from the building and paced the shaded concrete. Her stomach roiled. That's all Matt wanted from her, wasn't it? A dirty weekend away? Be the girl who entertained him in his new life as property manager and fawn over his many acres.

How the hell did her father think that she and Matt could ever be together?

'No thanks, Matt. Come up early all you like, but like I've told you, I'm not interested in rekindling anything. I'm seeing someone else now.'

Grace stilled. Panic clawed at her throat as her hand tightened around the phone. *Shit!* She wouldn't tell her best friends, but *Matt*? 'I mean—'

'So what?'

She blinked. 'So what?'

'Doesn't mean we still can't have fun. Is it serious?'

Grace could hardly believe what she was hearing. She opened her mouth. Closed it again.

'Well, think about it, Grace. I'll be up there anyway, so if—'

'No.' She cleared her throat, fire sparking inside her. 'I don't need to think about it. I don't know what impression I gave you—' or what her *father* had '—but I'm not that kind of girl. So please, Matt. Leave me alone.'

Grace hung up and, with a groan, dropped her face into her hands. Why would Matt even suggest such a thing? What was *wrong* with the men in her life?

Would she ever gain an ounce of respect?

* * *

Luke forced his hands to relax as he watched Grace stroll through the pub, her hair curtaining her face as she slid onto the stool beside Adam Maguire. The vice clenching his gut was uncalled for. She was spending time with her friend, that was all. Her friend who was being chatted up by the copper who was drinking with his mate.

The mate who was Grace's ex.

Gritting his teeth, Luke turned away, furious with himself

as he pulled another beer. He didn't care about them. Grace and Adam had been over for years and after Wednesday night, he was quite confident about where his relationship with Grace was going. He liked her. A lot. She was everything he thought she would be, and more. Her body fired like a rocket, strong and lithe beneath, beside, and above his. He hadn't been wrong about thinking she might be someone special. She was too special. But while he wanted to shout it from the rooftops, she wanted to keep the fact they were dating a secret.

He hated secrets.

Luke handed over the schooner, then turned to the next customer.

'Just a Tooheys, thanks, mate.'

He wrenched open the fridge and grabbed the beer. He needed to breathe. Relax. But he couldn't. He might be ready for dating and commitment, but was she? He didn't mind taking things slow and had meant what he'd said about Grace taking her time to tell people about them. But damn, it was hard not to stalk towards her, tip her back on the stool, and claim her sensual mouth with his.

Exhaling, he made change for the beer. Never mind. He was busy and had plenty to distract himself with as he worked his end of the bar. He didn't need to witness Cade Wilson flirting with his sister or Adam Maguire undoubtedly putting the moves on Grace. Luke didn't need to think about whether he trusted her. He did, heart and soul. She was a wholesome, down-to-earth woman and he liked so much about her. Except for that cloud that passed through her eyes at any mention of her family.

He scooped a glass of ice. What was it about them that bothered her? Why did she believe she had nothing to give in a relationship? Why didn't she want him to make a fuss of her and let her drink free for the evening? He could afford to lose the few bucks in Diet Coke.

Luke turned to the bistro bar and greeted the couple awaiting him. Never mind Grace. Her presence alone filled his chest with enough warmth to help pass the evening while he fetched more drinks and chatted with the regulars.

Then suddenly, a shiver coursed through him and he turned towards Jessica's end of the bar. His sister flipped beer caps and placed fresh bottles in front of Adam and Cade. A couple of young blondes slipped up beside them, but the tumble of caramel-chocolate waves he searched for was nowhere in sight.

Grace was gone.

Chapter Twelve

The last rays of daylight shot pink and gold across the darkening sky as Grace walked home. Despite the breeze rustling the rosy tulips, sweat trickled down her back as she strode along Abbott Street. Even after sunset, the heat rarely reduced in North Queensland, but Grace didn't mind the walk. She needed time to think. And breathe.

What the hell was wrong with Luke?

Hugging herself, she forced down the hurt. He hadn't looked at her once all afternoon. Everything had been going so well. Wednesday night had been fantastic, lasting into the early hours when Grace had crawled into her own bed at two am, aching and exhausted. She'd longed to stay, but despite the amazing sex, she hadn't wanted questions from her friends when they woke to find her bed hadn't been slept in. Luke had worked late last night, so they'd only sent each other text messages. Grace had hoped they could chat and laugh over the bar tonight before meeting him later after work.

But clearly, that wasn't going to happen.

Dropping her arms, she turned onto Jabiru Road and quickened her stride. Screw Luke. And screw Matt. She might have let too much slip during their conversation, and that he thought she was some kind of loose spirit who would simply fall back into bed with him made her long for a shower and to rub her skin raw.

But she'd been surer of her relationship with Luke. Dating him might be risky as all hell, but he was worth it.

Until he'd gone all iceman on her just because she was talking to an ex-boyfriend.

Exhaling between her teeth, Grace shot her hand through her hair. Hopefully, that wasn't the reason. Luke was far too secure to think such a thing. Adam might be notorious for his careless attitude and tendency to flirt with too many ladies, but the man was harmless! He was charming to the core and their conversation today could hardly be construed as flirting.

But whatever. She'd been keen to see Luke tonight and have all sorts of fun with him, but if he wanted to ignore her, it was his loss. At least she'd get some sleep.

Except she didn't. Grace lay awake for hours, staring up at the ceiling as she simmered over his actions. Her belly coiled, skin prickled, and she hated the annoyance pulsing through her. Luke shouldn't have such power over her feelings. Not yet.

She'd heard Jessica come in about an hour ago, so Luke must be home too. But she resisted the temptation to message him, closed her eyes, and focused on her breathing to calm her mind. She drifted to sleep, but the moment she woke, Luke and his ridiculous behaviour sent her pulse racing again. Grace groaned into her pillow. Dammit, she didn't need this. She wouldn't spend her day agitated and doubting herself. It wasn't like her. So, employing every mental tool she knew, Grace shoved Luke from her mind. She wasn't on call and therefore not rostered to work the Saturday morning, but she'd planned to go in for a few hours as she had ordering and care plan management to catch up on and Emma was running her Mums and Bubs clinic at ten o'clock. So, she buttoned up a crimson work shirt, grabbed her bag, and walked around the block to the surgery.

Beating Emma there, she switched on the air conditioners and settled down at the computer. Care planning wasn't her favourite task, but it wasn't hard to write a health summary, note observations, and organise referrals for patients to see the physiotherapist in Mareeba.

She'd just started the second letter when the surgery door opened and footsteps padded over the tiles. Rolling her chair back, Grace glanced through the door.

'Hi, Ed.' She stood and wandered into reception, greeting the middle-aged banana farmer. 'What brings you in?'

Ed leaned his forearm on the counter. 'Been having a bit of chest pain.'

Grace's instincts kicked in as she nodded and strode around the counter. 'All right. You're coming straight out the back with me.'

Patients could walk in with any array of problems, but the moment they uttered the words 'chest pain', anything else she was doing had to be set aside. Sometimes it was inconvenient, but today, she simply guided Ed into the treatment room. He didn't appear to be in any great distress. His breathing seemed normal and he had colour in his cheeks. Chest pain could be a symptom of many underlying causes, but it was always treated as a heart attack until proven otherwise.

'Take your shirt off and have a lie down,' she said, staying beside him until Ed lay comfortably on the treatment bed. 'Now, when did the pain start?'

'About twenty minutes ago. I was at the supermarket buying bread and thought I better come up here.'

She nodded and grabbed the ECG electrodes. 'At least you didn't ignore it.' So many people did. 'Where exactly is the pain? Left? Right?'

'Central chest.'

'And is it sharp? Crushing? Does it come and go?'

She stuck electrodes to each of his forearms, then his lower legs. Ed described the pain, what he'd been doing, and denied shortness of breath or dizziness. Grace palpated his intercostals to place the electrodes, then hooked up the ECG connections.

'Okay, Ed. Lie still and relax for me.'

She moved to the computer, opened the ECG software, and grabbed the phone. By the time Joanne answered, Grace was interpreting the reading and relating the case.

'ST segment is isoelectric in all leads,' she reported. 'P waves are present. Axis might be deviating slightly, but otherwise I'm seeing normal sinus rhythm.'

She paused the ECG, printed it, and saved it to Ed's chart.

'I'll be there in ten. Have a listen to his chest for me and see when he last had bloods done.'

'All right.' She ended the call and had a quick look at Ed's results, noting he'd hadn't had blood tests for five years. Not good for a man in his sixties, but not surprising either. For a single man who worked most days supervising on Shadow Creek, he hadn't been on top of his regular check-ups. But by the time Grace had finished working him up, his pain had gone, and Joanne had deemed there no reason to send him to Mareeba. Ed agreed he'd be back on Monday for blood tests.

'It's important to stay on top of these things, Ed,' Joanne

said kindly. 'I would recommend routine blood work in your age group so that we can catch any changes to your health and manage them before it gets too serious.'

'Rightio, doc. I can do that. Have never had any problems so I'll admit, the pain scared me a little.'

'And good for you for not just waiting for it to go away,' Grace said. 'You should never ignore chest pain.'

Ed left promising to call if the pain came back, then Grace returned to her care plans. They didn't write many, considering the lack of allied health support around Elizadale, but some people would drive to Cairns and health professionals occasionally visited Mareeba. But there wasn't enough work to bring them to Elizadale. One day, Grace would like to complete a post-graduate degree in diabetes education, which would be a great asset to the community, but having only just finished her training in x-ray and phlebotomy, she didn't want to overwhelm herself.

She finished her care planning, sent the monthly vaccine order to Queensland Health, then headed home for lunch. When Jessica returned from her shift at the pub, Grace and her friends did some yoga before getting ready for Carols by Candlelight.

Every year, Elizadale hosted carols in James Abbott Park on the corner of the highway and Riley Road. The football fields bordered the community centre and locals flocked with their picnic rugs to celebrate the holidays in song. A stage was set on the back of a truck, a barbeque drifted from the CWA tent, and everyone gathered to watch the school kids and their talented locals perform.

Claire, Jessica, and Grace wandered through the crowd, searching for Claire's family who they were to meet. The setting sun took most of its warmth with it as children ran around sporting Christmas shirts with Santa hats on or ribbons in their hair. Couples laughed, babies gurgled in prams, and a general merriment filled the air.

Grace smiled softly. This was what she loved about Christmas. She and her friends hadn't been shy about dressing up either, wearing Christmas singlets while Claire had braided ribbons through their hair. Jessica looked about twelve with two blonde braids hanging over her shoulders.

'Claire! Girls, over here!'

Claire's sister, Leanne Newman, waved them over from where she sat with her daughter, Faith, and sister-in-law, Rebecca Taylor.

'Hey! Hi, Faith!' Claire smiled at her niece. 'What have you got?'

'Candle! You should get one Aunty Claire!'

Grace smiled as she spread their blanket and sat beside Leanne. 'Where's Lisa?'

'She's running around with her friends,' Rebecca replied, nursing a bottle of water.

'And Jason and Joel?' Jessica asked, enquiring about their husbands.

'They ran into Jack and Adam on the way in,' Leanne replied. 'They'll be along shortly. Unless there's something new about banana farming one doesn't know about.'

'Any excuse to talk bananas,' Claire said, sitting cross-legged on their rug. 'So, should we get a sausage before the carols start?'

Grace and Leanne offered to do the food run and the ladies handed over their coins. Faith joined them as they crossed the park, the little girl chatting incessantly as six-year-olds did. But Grace barely heard a word as she scanned the crowd for any sign of her family. Her father wouldn't be there as he never attended community events, but her mother would undoubtedly seek her out. Then again, Grace could hardly avoid her if Zoe was coming because Zoe would want to see her sister, Rebecca.

The perils of small towns. Everyone knew each other or was married into someone else's family.

They ordered the food for their group and Grace opted for hot chips for lack of any beef-free choices. Faith dug straight into her sausage on bread as they returned to their blankets. Spotting the cascading dark curls sitting with her friends, Grace suppressed a groan. Zoe had found Rebecca and had brought Francesca with her.

'Grace!' Her mother grinned as Grace sat, handing sausages and chips to Claire and Jessica. 'There you are.'

Grace forced a smile. 'Hey.'

'Did Matt call you?'

Grace bit into a chip. No other greeting, not that she was surprised. Her parents would have undoubtedly known about the phone call or have encouraged him. And if that's what they wanted for her, to be Matt's Elizadale bed buddy, then it gave Grace all the more pleasure to disappoint them.

'Yep,' she said, cracking open her can of Diet Coke.

'And are you going to see him for New Year's?'

'No.'

Francesca's face fell. 'Why not? You should give him a chance, Grace.'

'He had one. And I've already told you, I'm not interested.'

Her mother had no chance to retort as Peter Harris, the usual emcee, welcomed everyone to the concert. Jason and Joel joined them and Grace was saved from Francesca resurrecting the subject of Matt as ladies who sang in the church choir opened the show. They performed two traditional carols, which Grace and her friends sang along to, then the school groups performed. Faith's grade one class sang 'Rudolf the Red Nose Reindeer' and Lisa's prep class entertained them with 'Jingle Bells'. Grace and her friends sang merrily while Rebecca and Leanne took photos and videoed their kids.

Once the school groups finished and the children had returned to the crowd to await Santa Claus, their local should-be country star, Meg Riley, graced the stage. Her beautiful soprano voice filled their hearts with her rendition of 'Silent Night' before she belted out the more upbeat 'Come O Ye Faithful'. Cheering with the rest of the crowd, Grace almost missed it as her phone beeped. Peter announced the next performer as Grace glanced at the message. It was from Luke. Frowning, she considered ignoring it. His hurtful behaviour last night had almost become a forgotten memory as the day had flashed by, but her restless heart had other ideas.

Hope you're enjoying the carols. I'll be working late but we could go for coffee at the roadhouse later. Or something.

Grace scoffed. 'Or something'. Yeah, she knew what that meant. Ignore her one night, then booty call her the next? Humph, maybe she was mad at him after all. Sure, he might have been busy, but he still could have said hello to her after everything they'd got up to in his bedroom the other night.

Taking a deep belly breath, she slid her phone back into her pocket. She was sick of being taken for granted, so she'd reply to his message when she had something nice to say. Deep down, she knew he wouldn't have intentionally hurt her. Luke wasn't like Matt or her father. And she wanted to see him tonight. She wanted to talk to him. Kiss him. Spend more time wrapped in his brawny arms.

Heat coiled inside her and Grace clutched the picnic blanket. She didn't want to shut him out.

When Francesca left to fetch herself a drink and the little girls were jumping around to 'Six White Boomers', Zoe scooted closer to Grace.

'I heard what happened between you and Matt. I'm sorry your parents are being harsh about it.'

Shoving her frustrations aside, Grace glanced at Zoe. Grace had always liked her and as far as sisters-in-law went, she could do a lot worse.

'Can't change them now. I just refuse to be used in a business deal, which, knowing my father, I'm sure is involved somehow.'

'Yeah, Charlie was a little miffed too, thinking Matt was good for you. I told him to leave it alone, that it wasn't his business.'

'Thank you.'

'As long as you're happy, don't let them influence you.'

'I won't. And I am happy. I'm … I don't need Matt.'

Excited shrieks shot across the park, ending that conversation as Peter announced that Santa Claus was coming. Lisa and Faith jumped up and down, piercing Grace's eardrums.

'But if we want him to know where we are, we need to keep singing!' Peter said as he announced their actually-made-it country stars, The Charlie Boys—Chaz, Chuck, and Charles—to the stage to entertain them with Aussie Christmas songs in true country fashion. Meg soon joined them—Chaz was her cousin—and captivated the crowd with 'Hark! The Herald Angels Sing'.

Afterwards, Grace pulled her phone from her pocket and

replied to Luke. **Sure. Text me when you leave and I'll meet you at your place.**

She wanted to see him. It was simple as that. She might be mad, but unlike her parents, she wouldn't go into a misunderstanding with her guns blazing. That sort of attitude wasn't helpful for a healthy relationship. She'd simply ask him why he hadn't acknowledged her and see what he had to say.

Chapter Thirteen

The Christmas tree lights cast a multi-coloured glow over the lounge room as Luke Bluetoothed his phone to the speaker and set the volume down low. Sometimes he wondered why he bothered assembling a tree every year when all the presents went straight to his parents' house, but Christmas was hardly festive without tinsel around the windows, decorative homewares on the table, and a fake green pine tree covered in shiny ornaments.

Luke glanced around the lounge room. The lights and soft country music added a romantic ambiance that, while subtle, he hoped wasn't too much. He didn't want to scare Grace off.

Shoving his hand through his damp hair, he blew out a deep breath. He hadn't a clue what was going on with him. He might have liked her for a long time, but could he already be in love with her? Did it matter that they'd only been 'dating' for a week? Who said there needed to be a timeframe? Were you physically incapable of falling in love until the three-month mark? Six months? Of course not.

He couldn't get her off his mind. After spending the morning decorating the house, he'd left for work. Saturdays always kept him busy and he hated that a midnight date was all he could offer Grace, but he'd needed to see her. When she'd accepted, he'd shut the bar down as soon as he could, left the paperwork for Monday, and had rushed home to shower off the stench of sweat and beer. Mango sorbet was setting in the freezer and he couldn't possibly have overdone the ambiance with only a Christmas tree, Lee Kernaghan strumming his guitar, and the Cowboys cheering on the wall with the Provan-Summons Trophy.

A knock sounded and his spine stiffened. Too late to change anything now. Crossing the room, Luke pulled open the door.

Everything stopped.

Yeah, he was in love. His breath catching in his throat and everything vanishing from his vision except Grace was an obvious sign and symptom. She stood with her hand on her hip in a clingy green T-shirt and denim shorts, pink rubber thongs on her feet. She wore her hair twisted up in a complicated braid only Claire could have done with red and green ribbon threaded through her brown locks. An odd sparkle filled her eyes, one that her mouth didn't mimic as she jingled the keys in her hand. She carried nothing else.

Luke swallowed the lump in his throat. 'You look … gorgeous.'

He longed to take her in his arms and greet her with a hot kiss, but instead, he stepped back and gestured her inside like a gentleman before closing both doors behind her.

'Thank you,' she replied, her gaze straying around the room. 'How was work?'

'Busy enough, but I think carols stole most of the crowd.' He reached for her, needing to have her in his arms. It'd been far too many nights apart for a relationship so new.

But Grace moved out of his reach and towards the kitchen, leaving him frowning as his hands dropped back to his sides. She placed her keys on the bench, then turned to face him, her eyes hot.

'Luke, I want to talk about last night.'

'Last night?'

'Yes.' She paused, swallowed, then let out a deep breath. 'Look, I'm not opposed to sneaking over here at this hour because you work most nights. And I know I said I didn't want to tell anyone about us right now. But I don't see how that gives you any excuse to behave as you did.'

Luke stared at her. She was mad. Or hurt, he wasn't sure which, but panic rose in his throat just the same as he resisted the urge to scratch his head. What had he done wrong? She'd been at the pub … Cade and Adam had been there … she'd been absolutely stunning in her red and white dress and he'd tried his best to stay away—

Slapping his hands to his eyes, Luke groaned. Seeing his actions from her point of view, bile filled his mouth. 'Shit, Grace. I'm sorry.'

Unrooting his feet, he strode towards her. Grace remained where she was, her arms crossed and eyes dark. But he risked it anyway and placed his hands on her small shoulders.

Her eyebrow quirked. 'Whatever for?'

'For avoiding you. I … I ignored you and it wasn't right.'

'No. It wasn't.'

Despite her hurt, she remained composed while his guts twisted at his actions. Not being able to flirt with her last night had annoyed him and sent him into a bad mood because he hadn't been sure about their relationship. He'd realised he was falling for her and longed to know why she hesitated. But just because she wasn't ready to tell people, that didn't mean he couldn't have at least said hello.

Closing the distance between them, Luke brushed his hands down her slender arms. Her eyes thawed, and the tightness in his chest eased. 'I'm sorry. I don't know what I was thinking.'

Seconds passed as her chocolatey eyes bored into his. Luke didn't dare move. Then she sighed, dropped her crossed arms, and wrapped them around his waist.

'It's okay. I wasn't too … well, I was upset. Annoyed more than anything. But please don't ignore me, Luke. I don't like it.'

'I'm sorry.' He could hardly believe he'd done such a thing and hated that he'd hurt her. Drawing her close, he rested his cheek on top of her pretty head. 'I didn't mean to. I won't do it again.'

'Thank you. I didn't think you did it on purpose.'

'Never. I'd just been over the books, which never makes me happy, and Bill hadn't liked my suggestion of taking garlic bread off the menu. Then when I saw you in Jessica's section, I just … you send me crazy, Grace. You don't know how beautiful you are. All I wanted to do was kiss you and shower you with free drinks, but I knew you wouldn't like that.'

She lifted her head and smiled, running her hands up and down his back. 'Not right now, but one day soon. I promise. I'm just not ready for the questions and I like the little bubble we're in.'

'Me too.' Although the sooner it burst, the better. 'Next time, I'll absolutely say hello to you.'

'That's all I ask. Now, it's late and I think we've done enough talking.'

She rose onto her toes and kissed him, running her hands down his butt and urging him a step closer. Luke didn't hesitate, following Grace's lead as her lips parted and he dived in, ravishing her until neither of them could breathe. But he didn't care for oxygen right now. Running his hands around her waist, he went on an expedition for red and lifted her shirt up over her head, breaking their kiss long enough to glance down. Seeing the black encasing her beautiful skin, his blood heated.

'You're not on call, are you?'

'Nuh-uh.'

'Good. Bedroom?'

'Lounge.'

He raised his eyebrows. 'Really?'

Her eyes glittered. 'I like the Christmas tree. It's pretty and I've always been a sucker for fairy lights.'

'I knew I put it up for a reason.'

He took her hand and led her to the lounge. Grace pressed her hands to his shoulders, urged him to sit, and Luke fell onto the cushions. His hands caressed her thighs as she knelt over him and snaked her hands beneath his shirt. He shivered at her touch, flexed his abs, and grinned as she moaned.

Grace grabbed the hem of his shirt and he helped her lift it off. Her dark eyes soaked him in before her shoulders softened and she pressed her mouth to his. Luke grabbed her hips, groaning as her bra grazed his chest. Damn, he liked lace. Running his hands up over her waist and ribs, he moulded her bra. Her nipples hardened, but he didn't linger, moving to slip his fingers into her luscious hair.

Frustration coursed through him when he remembered she'd tied it up. 'Dammit.'

Breathless, Grace broke their kiss as she pulled at the knots in her hair. Two long braids fell over her shoulders. Her hands made quick work of one braid and Luke reached for the other, her hair running like silk through his fingers as the strands unfurled. They dropped the ribbons to the floor and he brushed his hands through her long, caramel-coloured tendrils.

'Damn, you're beautiful.'

She stared at him for what seemed like an eternity. His heart hammered as shadows passed through her eyes. What was she thinking? Was that worry he sensed? Apprehension? His gut clenched.

Then her mouth lowered back to his and all thought slipped away as she brushed her lips against his. He relished the moment, enjoying the tenderness as an ache squeezed around his heart. Then she drew his lower lip between her teeth and the heat returned. The buckle of his shorts opened.

'Grace ... all the condoms are in the bedroom.'

Blowing out her breath, she rose from the lounge and shimmied out of her tiny denim shorts. Luke's mouth dried as she stood gloriously in her black lace underwear and brushed her dishevelled hair over her shoulders as the Christmas tree illuminated her creamy skin in a festive glow.

All the remaining blood drained from his head.

'Same spot?' she asked.

He nodded. Grace turned and strode away, her hips swaying in her scrappy knickers. He must have been a really good boy this year to have received her for Christmas. Though what he'd done, he hadn't a clue.

Gathering himself, he pulled off his shorts and kicked them towards the rest of their clothes as Grace raced back into the room. She dropped the box on the ground and tore open a packet, but before she could go any further, Luke sat forward, hooked a finger through either side of her lace knickers, and pulled her close.

He let his gaze wander, taking his time to soak her in and appreciate her delicate beauty. She truly was gorgeous. Running his hands up her slender torso, he traced the inner line of her ribcage. She wasn't muscular but had honed a taut body with slender aerobic muscles. And as the reds, greens, yellows, and blues danced across her pale skin, he knew without a doubt that she was the gift he'd always wanted wrapped sensually in black lace.

Grace's hands fell to his shoulders as his thumbs brushed the underwire of her bra, before fluttering down her back. The taut muscles on either side of her spine rippled. Her knickers hid nothing and rode low on her hips. He swallowed hard, his heart hammering as his hands ran over her shapely butt.

Then he slipped his hands beneath the lace, cupped her glutes, and pressed a kiss to her belly. Her fingers dug into his shoulders as he tasted her skin, hot, sweet, and sensual against his tongue. She shivered and his hands hardened. Moving lower, he let everything go as he tasted, kissed, and sucked at her skin until his lips found the lace. Her body jerked and he toyed with her until she all but shuddered on her feet, crying out softly.

'Luke … God, I can't …'

Tearing his face away, he withdrew his hands and slipped her knickers down her legs. As she stepped out of them, he wrapped his arms around her and pulled her down, her knees straddling him as her breasts pressed against his chest. He didn't tear his gaze from hers, drowsy with pleasure.

'I think I've found something I like better than the red.'

She pressed her forehead against his. 'Black lace. Works every time.'

'For good reason.' He unclasped her bra and she dropped it to the floor, her nipples hard and breasts tender against his skin. Glancing at the condom in her hand, she bit down on her lip.

'Um … I think I punctured it with my fingernail …'

A laugh tore from his gut, his shoulders shaking as he tightened his hold on her. 'Hold on.'

With his hand on her back, he bent over. Grace's arms tightened around his neck, her hair brushing the carpet as he reached for the box on the floor. Bringing her back upright, he offered it to her. Tossing the broken one aside, she reached for another and wasted no time in prepping him, her hands hot and soft against his heated flesh. Luke inhaled, his grip on her hips tightening.

Good God, no woman had ever made him feel this way. She didn't even know how much power she wielded or what a temptress she really was.

His hands brushed up her back and into her hair. 'Now I'm glad I put the tree up.'

The freckles over her nose crinkled. 'Why?'

'You look beautiful in this light.'

'I think you need your eyes checked.' Laughing, she pushed his shoulders against the lounge and lowered herself over him.

He inhaled sharply, feeling every inch of her as she took him in. He grabbed her butt and pulled her closer, allowing her to sink fully before running his hands up her body. Her arms weakened, but she continued to seize control and led them through it. He dipped his head and placed his lips against her neck, her pulse throbbing beneath his kiss.

She gasped as his hands went to her breasts. They weren't big but filled his hands perfectly as he teased her nipples until she moaned.

'Oh, God, Luke.'

Lowering his head, he thrust against her again, holding her deep as he nipped at her throat. She rolled her hips and Luke groaned, his teeth scraping along her skin as a shock ran from his groin to his heart.

The moment seemed to last forever. He kissed her everywhere, his fingers playing below her waist until she perspired and broke into a climax. His hands squeezed her thighs to hold her in position.

Then something dark rose inside him and, needing more, he flipped her onto the lounge. She didn't hesitate as her legs wrapped around his waist and he dug his knees in, set to bring them both to an entirely different ending as he closed his mouth over hers.

They swallowed each other's cries.

* * *

Grace could hardly breathe with Luke's ridiculously heavy weight pressing over her, but she never wanted to move. She could die right there and die happy. She never needed to have sex again unless it could beat that. If it did, it'd probably kill her.

Somewhere in the room, Adam Harvey sang about beer while the Christmas lights danced on the ceiling. Grace couldn't tear her eyes from them. She'd noticed the effort Luke had put in when she'd arrived, finding the place a little more seductive. The tree provided soft, glowing light and he had a damn fine taste in music. Although she couldn't believe she'd just had extraordinary earth-shattering sex surrounded by the deep smooth serenade of Garth Brooks.

Exhaling, she lifted her hand to her sweaty forehead.

'I'm sorry,' Luke breathed, and she turned her gaze to meet his, their heads resting close on the arm of the lounge. 'I lost control there.'

Smiling softly, she placed her hand on his stubbly cheek. 'Are you serious? It was brilliant. I just can't believe you had it in you.'

Luke lifted himself up and gazed down at her, a wicked grin curving his mouth. 'Exercise builds more than just muscle mass.'

'And you have plenty of that. But seriously …' She exhaled. 'Aren't you hot?'

'Bloody sweating, as you can tell.'

Running her hands down his shoulders, she gripped his rock-hard biceps. 'Maybe we should have a shower.'

'Only if you stay.'

Her pulse spiked. 'Stay?'

'Yeah.' Luke brushed his finger down her cheek, silver flittering through his azure eyes. Grace softened, her toes curling into the lounge. 'It's almost one in the morning, Grace. I was dead on my feet and have no idea how I managed to do that, but we are sticky and sweaty, so a shower is in order. And you live so far away.'

She bit down on her lower lip to stop herself from grinning. 'It's a one minute drive.'

'Come on.' His lips curved in a smile she couldn't refuse. 'Stay with me. I'll make you breakfast and orgasm in the morning.'

What choice did a girl have? Grinning, Grace wrapped her arms around his neck and gave him a smacking kiss. 'Okay.'

Untangling themselves from the lounge, Luke led her into

the bathroom. Grace yawned, exhausted as he tested the water. After a moment, he pulled her with him beneath the spray and the door clattered closed behind them.

Her hot skin cooled as Luke held her close and stooped to rest his forehead against hers. She looped her arms around his hips and rested her hands on the globes of his tight butt. Water plastered her hair to her shoulders and a smooth hum radiated through her body. She never wanted to move from here either. Standing with Luke … just holding each other … all her worries washed down the drain with their sweat. As his hands brushed up and down her spine, she closed her eyes and inhaled his salty scent while they wasted precious water.

After an age, she asked, 'Um … are we going to wash or just get wet?'

'We'll wash. I just enjoy holding you.'

Smiling softly, she turned her head and kissed his biceps, before resting her cheek against his shoulder and yawning. This was too nice. Intimate and lovely. Too much for their 'just dating' status?

Grace tightened her grip around him. She could stay here forever if—

'Yeah, we really shouldn't be wasting water.' Luke straightened, and Grace's eyes snapped open as he reached for the soap. They washed, then he pulled her back into his arms. Sleepy and sated, Luke kissed her slowly before turning off the water. They stepped out of the cubicle.

'You don't have a towel. Wait a sec.'

Luke ran from the room dripping wet, leaving her giggling until he returned with a fluffy green towel. She dried herself off and wrung out her hair before wrapping the towel around her body. In the bedroom, Luke rummaged through the drawer for a set of pyjamas and tossed her the T-shirt. It read

'Mornings are for Coffee' and she smiled as he pulled on a pair of coffee-printed shorts.

'We match.'

He grinned. 'We do.'

Ignoring the ball of warmth threatening her heart, Grace slipped the shirt over her head. It fell to her knees and over one shoulder, but it didn't matter. She slid beneath the covers as Luke collapsed onto his back and threw his arms above his head. Grace hugged his waist and pillowed her head on his bare chest, snuggling in close. He switched off the lamp and with his arm around her, Grace closed her eyes with a smile. Emma had been right. Dating did carry the risk of developing deeper feelings, and there sure was potential for her falling in love with Luke. A terrifying prospect when he wasn't a cattleman. Oh, the things her father would do. He'd lie. Manipulate. She would lose Luke. Edward would turn him away from her and—

His arm tightened around her, and Grace exhaled. Warm and snug, she wouldn't worry. She would stand up for Luke and he wouldn't take an ounce of her father's bullshit.

She hoped.

Chapter Fourteen

The pencil snapped in Edward's clenched fist. He was going to blow. That bloody daughter of his was ruining everything! She had no respect for him or her family. And because of her pig-headedness, Matt Clark was threatening to call off their deal.

'I thought we had this settled, White.' Matt's hard voice vibrated through the phone and Edward's hand clenched around the receiver as he sat in his dingy office. 'But Grace doesn't seem as loose and gold-digging as you suggested and seems set against me. Now, I'll happily provide you with my bull, but only family get him at the discounted price. *Heavily* discounted.'

Edward gritted his teeth and flung the pencil across the room. He couldn't lose this deal. He'd spent his life trying to get White Peaks back on track, ever since the local farmers had banded together to uncover his father's fraud and sully his family's name. So what if his father had doctored a few books? It's not like any of them hadn't done it or hid money from the tax agent or written off personal items as a business expense.

The world was a tough place and a man needed to do whatever he could to get ahead.

In the decades since, he'd fixed most of the mess his father had left him with. But a desperate man did whatever it took, and Wagyu beef was the way to go. That bull was vital to his plan, but Edward couldn't afford the fee that the Clarks were asking.

If Grace had to pay the price, so be it. The least she could do was marry Matt. Why would that be such a burden? She'd have a rich husband and a wealth of property far greater than he could ever imagine. Since when had women stopped doing what they were damn well told?

'I'll talk to her again, Clark. Grace is easy. I'm sure once you get here you could sweep her back into your bed and she'll beg for a ring on her finger.'

'You'd think,' he snickered. 'But your daughter has already moved on. Said she was seeing someone. There's no use pursuing a woman when there are plenty of others out there, so it seems your chance is finished, mate.'

Edward's jaw clenched. Grace was seeing someone? How had that got under his radar? Who was this bastard? He knew everything that went on in this town. It was something he privately boasted about.

'Don't count on it, Clark. Grace's little flings are never serious.'

'You just call me when things change or if you want Wally at the service price. Either way, talk to your daughter. With the union between our properties, there can be significant benefits, White. For both of us. So do what you need to do and get it done!'

Matt hung up. Swearing, Edward slammed the phone back

into the cradle and shoved out of his chair. His heart pounded as he paced his office.

If only Grace wasn't hell bent on defying him. Bloody useless woman with her head in the fucking clouds. He was her father and knew what was best. If someone else had caught her eye, he'd need to rectify that. Quickly.

It didn't matter who the bloke was, there was no one in the region Edward deemed more suitable for Grace than Matt. This mystery man was nothing more than a bug that needed to be squashed.

* * *

Luke woke but didn't dare open his eyes. The blankets lay snug over his chest, the room cool thanks to the air conditioner he rarely slept with, light barely blinking through his bedroom blinds. Heat from the small, gorgeous body lying beside his kept him warm and it took all his strength not to leap for joy.

Grace White was in his bed, her arm around his waist and smooth leg tucked between his. Her head had moved from his chest to the pillow during the night and by the sound of her breathing, she was still asleep on his arm. It had lost all feeling. He flexed his hand and resisted a wince as pins and needles shot up his forearm. Peeking his eyes open, he turned to her and his pulse spiked.

There was no going back now. If he could wake to her beautiful face every day for the rest of his life, he'd die a happy man. Her hair hung over her shoulder and spread across his pale blue pillow. Grace slept peacefully, her lashes long against her creamy cheeks. He wanted to kiss every single one of the cute freckles on her nose. Her delectable lips parted slightly, moist and plump. Luke longed to taste them but didn't dare. He couldn't disturb her. He would be content to watch her for however long it took for Grace to wake.

His heart swelled with both fear and comfort. He was ready for this. For her. He wanted everything. There was nothing holding him back. He had his career on track and knew what he wanted out of life. He had a supportive family and good friends. So, it had been far from inconvenient when Grace had sashayed into the pub—as she had so many times before—and finally captured his heart.

He had a lot to thank the new menu for. He'd sparked her interest and lured her in with the temptation of food, only to have her discover what he'd always hoped—that they possessed more heat than the kitchen.

Sometimes, it felt strange that he hadn't noticed her long ago. They'd lived in Elizadale their whole lives. But being four years older than her, he'd hardly given her a second look when she'd been at his house playing with Jessica as a child. He had almost graduated Mareeba High when she'd started there, then he'd spent a few years working around Australia in other pubs. But they'd both been living in Elizadale as mostly single adults for a few years now and while he'd considered her pretty for most of that time, never had he thought he'd discover feelings this deep.

She was the one. There was no doubt about it. And that scared him to bits because she didn't seem ready for the level of commitment that he wanted.

Sighing, Luke lifted his free hand to his forehead. He needed to talk to her. Find out what was holding her back. He couldn't risk sharing his feelings, at least not right now. She was the one who had suggested they keep things casual. He'd told her he was easy going, but that had been before his heart was involved.

Now, he'd risk everything for her.

Luke didn't know how long he lay there and may have drifted back to sleep. But next thing he knew, Grace's arm tightened around his waist as she exhaled an incredibly cute morning sigh. He watched her stretch, her nose crinkling adorably before she opened her eyes. Her lashes fluttered and her big chocolate irises met his.

Smiling, he caressed her naked hip. 'Good morning.'

She returned his smile sleepily, running her hand over his rumbling belly. 'Morning. How long have you been awake?'

'Not long. How'd you sleep?'

'Great. What's the time?'

'Got somewhere to be?' Laughing, Luke reached for his phone.

'No, just wondering how mad Jess and Claire—'

'Shit!' Luke's eyebrows shot up as he stared at his phone. 'It's twelve-forty-five!'

'In the afternoon!'

He met her wide-eyed gaze. 'We must have been tired.'

'Well, I wore you out. So much for making me breakfast.'

'Yeah, you did wear me out.' There was no doubt about that as he placed his phone down and moved until he lay over her. 'But I can still make you pancakes.'

'Hmm … pancakes sound good.'

Thankfully, despite the time, neither of them had anywhere to be. Grace ran her hands up his back as he kissed her softly. Toying with her tongue, he drew on her lips until his heart ached. She arched, her breasts pressing against his chest, nipples hard with arousal as her thighs tightened around him.

Drawing away, he watched her eyes flutter open and a cheeky grin curve the corners of her mouth. 'You also promised me an orgasm.'

Laughing, Luke ran his hand down her body and then crept beneath his T-shirt to caress her breast. 'Oh, Grace. I will. But honestly, I need food first.'

He rolled away and took her hand, loving her even more when she laughed and followed him to the kitchen.

* * *

After a pancake breakfast for lunch and a quick return to bed, Grace thought it best she went home. At the door, Luke's hands fell to her hips and he brushed his lips over hers.

'Have a good afternoon. I'm working late tomorrow, but I'll finish early on Tuesday if you want to do something. I knock off at five.'

She ran her hands up his back, ignoring the part of her that longed to stay. 'I'll pop by after that as I work until five too.'

He kissed her again, lingering long enough to make her toes curl. No, she couldn't stay. Nothing was stopping her, but she couldn't make their relationship just about sex. She wanted things to grow deeper. More serious. God help her.

'Bye, Luke.'

'Bye, Grace.' He opened the door and she stepped out into the humid afternoon. 'I'll call or message you tomorrow.'

She grinned. 'Try to keep them clean.'

'You know I can't promise that.'

Laughing, she crossed to the car, climbed in, and waved before driving away. As she turned up Stuart Road, her hands tightened around the wheel as she anticipated what awaited her at home. Her friends had sent many text messages throughout the morning, some filled with worry while others contained a touch of hurt mixed with good humour, such as Claire's, **He better be damn good in bed, that's all I have to say. And if you snuck out to do anything but get laid, then there's something seriously wrong with you. Let me know you're okay.**

Guilt had gnawed at her insides and continued to churn she turned into Jackson Villas. But how could she look her best friend of almost twenty years in the eye and tell her she was sleeping with her brother?

Grace cringed and shut off the ignition. She'd have to find the courage because there was no way she could walk inside and avoid the subject. It would be awkward, but she wanted to share with her friends the excitement that fluttered in her belly every time she thought about Luke.

Taking a deep breath, she crossed the sunny driveway and entered the unit. Jessica sat curled up on the lounge, a book tucked into her lap. She glanced up, flipping her long blonde hair over her shoulder. 'Well, *hello* there. What have you been up to?'

Grace stifled a laugh. 'Hey, Jess. What are you reading?'

She held up a fantasy romance Grace hadn't seen before but that looked intriguing. 'Another indie author I'm loving.'

'And that Isabella recommended?' Isabella Brennan was the resident bookworm and conveniently lived next door.

'Of course. Now, don't avoid the subject.'

Sighing, Grace sat on the lounge next to Jessica's. 'I didn't mean to. It's just … I don't …'

'You're dating someone, Grace. After our discussion while putting up the tree, I was surprised, but I'm glad too. I just don't know why you're sneaking around.'

'I didn't mean to sneak around. And it has only been a

week. It's just … I wasn't sure how you … I mean …' Grace shook her head. Best to spit it out. 'I'm dating Luke.'

The book fell into Jessica's lap as her eyebrows shot up. 'What? Luke? My brother Luke?'

'Yeah.'

Jessica blinked her big blue eyes. Grace's heart pounded. Belly clenched. Could Jessica say something?

'It just happened, Jess. I said something about dating, and Emma said he was hot. Then I was talking to him about the menu and he invited me to dinner to try some of his ideas and really … he's such a nice guy.'

'He's a big muscley dork!'

Grace choked back a laugh. 'Of course, you think so, but I—'

'Oh my God!' Leaping out of her chair, Jessica bounced down onto the lounge beside Grace, grinning ear to ear. 'This is awesome! Do you really like him?'

Grace's spine relaxed. 'Yeah. I do.'

'Oh, that's so weird,' Jessica muttered, shaking her head. Then she grabbed Grace's hand and squeezed. 'You must tell me everything! Not the part a sister doesn't want to know, but the other stuff.'

Grinning, Grace gave her friend the PG version, telling her about the night of the Christmas party and the few that followed.

'He sure knows how to cook, I can tell you that. And kiss.'

Jessica's nose wrinkled. 'Ew. But yes, he can cook. And I'm so glad!' She wriggled with glee. 'I want to see you happy, Grace. And Luke too. I love him, even though he's a pain in the arse sometimes. So, is it serious?'

She wanted it to be, but she couldn't shake her dread. Her heart pounded as though she'd just done a dozen sun salutations. But despite her fears, she didn't want Luke going anywhere. The pull between them was real. The moment Emma had pointed him out, a magnet had latched onto her heart, drawing her to the ironman she couldn't resist. And she was glad she hadn't, as she'd enjoyed getting to know him as more than Jessica's brother. She liked that he had a solid head on his shoulders and a sense of humour. He was friendly and close to his family, which she both appreciated and envied. And if last night was any indication, he cared about her. They had chemistry that wouldn't quit, and the mere thought of him put a pleasurable hum in her blood.

Exhaling, she looked Jessica in the eye and shrugged. 'Maybe?'

Jessica squealed and clapped her hands together before sighing and relaxing into the lounge. 'Oh, I'm so jealous. I wish Cade would ask me out.'

Grace placed her hand on Jessica's shoulder. 'He will. I'm sure of it. Now, I want to get changed and do some yoga. Do you want to join me?'

Jessica nodded, so they both changed and returned to the lounge room for savasana. Grace needed it. Lying on the living room floor in corpse pose, she tried to relax. She focused on her breathing and on emptying her mind.

But Luke wouldn't budge, which rendered savasana useless. Grace's hands curled against the mat. Waking with Luke this morning had been nothing short of wonderful. And had cemented her fear of falling in love with him.

But was it fear? The feelings swarming through her might rattle her nerves, but after waking in his arms to find him gazing at her, her pulse hadn't stopped pounding. She couldn't be *in* love with him. Their relationship might be fun and exciting, but it was far too new. And some things were still lacking. They'd become intimate on a physical level, but there was so much she didn't know about Luke. Nor had she shared her deepest demons with him.

Besides, neither of them had talked about the future. She might have pictured herself married with kids, but at twenty-four, Grace didn't want to start that any time soon. He might be four years older than her, but he'd just taken over the running of the pub and had goals of his own.

Opening her eyes, Grace hugged her knees to her chest, encouraging Jessica to do the same as she stared at the ceiling.

Then, as though reading her mind, Jessica asked, 'What are you going to do about your father?'

Anxiety rose in Grace's throat. Her heart pounded. 'I don't know.'

She couldn't keep Luke a secret forever. The moment Edward realised how important Luke was to her, he would ruin them for sure.

'Well, please be careful, Grace. I think Luke can handle your father, but we know how unpredictable Edward can be. I don't want to see Luke, or you, get hurt.'

Grace lifted her feet and gripped her big toes, her knees near her ears as she relaxed in happy baby. 'Me neither.'

Her father's wrath was inevitable, but hopefully she could control when it was unleashed. Until then, she relaxed into her stretch and told herself not to worry.

She could handle this.

By the time they'd finished stretching, Grace felt a lot calmer sitting with Jessica on the lounge talking books. When Claire arrived home from her trip to Tropic Sun, Grace shared her news with her too. Claire was even more excited than Jessica, shrieking as she sat on Grace's other side and begged for details.

'He has to be good, right? I mean, he's sweet and all, but is he as powerful and dominating as he is at the pub? And that body … oh my God, I can't believe you've been under that!'

'Um, hello!' Jessica waved her hands around her head. 'Sister right here!'

Grace laughed, leaning towards Claire while Jessica groaned and covered her ears. 'He's bloody perfect.'

Squealing, Claire wrapped her arms around Grace. 'I'm so happy for you! I mean, Jessica and I were bitching about you not telling us who you were dating and we came up with some possibilities. But we didn't consider Luke.'

Jessica's nose twisted. 'Of course not.'

'But this is seriously great!'

Grace wrapped her arms around her friends. 'I love you two.'

'We love you,' Claire said, leaning her head on Grace's shoulder. 'But don't keep secrets from us again, okay?'

Her guilt having subsided, Grace simply smiled. 'I won't. I promise.'

Chapter Fifteen

Bill placed the pumpkin burger down and rubbed his mouth with the back of his hand. Luke watched the cook as he contemplated the food. He'd spent hours last night finalising his ideas, writing a draft menu, printing the recipes, and organising a stock plan to present to Bill as they needed to get a move on if they were to launch on New Year's.

Bill cleared his throat. 'Yeah, that's pretty all right. Recipe seems easy enough too. I think I can manage it.'

Grinning, Luke resisted slapping the cook on the back. 'Thanks, mate. Does this mean you're on board?'

Bill shrugged and took another bite. 'You're the boss, boss man. And your idea's not a bad one. I've found the menu dull for years, but I'm a fan of the simple things. Although, I don't know how the locals will react.'

Luke leaned his hip against the steel counter. 'We're not doing anything out of the ordinary. The menu will simply offer a variety of meals that they can't get elsewhere in town. We can't compete if we serve the same food as the Royal.'

'That's true. So, if you want to replace the garlic bread with flatbread and dips, then I'm fine with that. But you know what I think we should have?'

'What's that?'

'Those sweet potato wedges. Don't worry, I can air fry them. But I had some in Cairns the other day and they were bloody delish.'

'We can do that,' he said, grateful that Bill wanted to contribute. 'We can have them as a starter and a side option.'

'And I reckon we grill the mackerel with garlic and paprika.'

'If you like.'

Bill enjoyed another bite of his burger, then extended his hand. 'All right, mate. Let's do this.'

Luke took Bill's hand and clapped him on the shoulder, unable to contain his grin. 'You won't be sorry.'

At five o'clock, Luke handed over the reins to Jessica and the casuals before striding home with a spring in his step. Bill was on board and Jessica had been right about this quarter's financials. Everything was going to be fine. He'd already spoken to Vicki at the bakery and would confirm with her this week about adjusting their order to include ciabatta bread and sourdough. Then he'd call Jade Farm and secure the deal to purchase their less-than-commercial quality avocados. Jessica would complete the menu design by giving it her artistic flare and they'd be ready to present it to their parents when they returned from their caravanning this weekend.

His dad might never have doubted him and had given him free rein, but Luke still hoped he'd be proud.

Halfway home, Luke's phone buzzed, and his heart flipped at Grace's name on the screen. **Sorry, stuck at work. Might be half an hour late.**

Luke's stomach sank. She must have an emergency and

couldn't help that, but he couldn't wait to tell her that Bill had come around.

No worries. See you later.

At least he'd have time for a workout. Pulling the door closed behind him, he switched on the air-conditioner and kicked off his work shoes. Despite the questions lurking in his mind, he liked where things were with Grace. But even though she'd told her friends yesterday, she remained adamant about keeping their relationship quiet, so he'd hesitated when he'd almost broached the subject with Joe. He didn't want to do that again. He wanted them to be a proper couple.

But that discussion was for later. Right now, he needed to relax and work off his excitement. Stripping off his work clothes, he pulled on a pair of shorts and he tied up his shoes. It was too humid to bother with a shirt as he grabbed a water bottle from the fridge. Heading out to the undercover patio, he jumped onto the treadmill.

* * *

Grace arrived at Luke's house determined to shove questions about their relationship aside. They'd only been dating for a week. Wasn't the fact that they liked each other all that mattered? It was Christmas, the season to be jolly. Not to worry.

Grace stepped inside the cool duplex. 'Hey, Luke!'

He didn't reply. Strolling through the unit, she called out again and dropped her bag onto the kitchen bench. Then she heard music playing outside.

What was he doing out there in this heat?

Sliding open the door, she stepped onto the patio. And halted. Luke was doing chin-ups. Knees bent, ankles crossed, doing chin-ups with what appeared to be such ease. His muscles rippled and bulged, breath exhaling every time his chin hit the bar. Grace's hand grabbed the wall as the blood drained from her head. Heat ignited inside her. Goddamn, he was ripped. Forget intimacy. Forget where this was going. All she wanted was him.

She didn't know how many chin-ups he'd done. It could have been two, it could have been ten. Who could count when mesmerised by such a magnificent back? His traps contracted and abducted, his triceps clenched tight, his deltoids bulged. Sweat trickled down his spine, creating a wet patch at the top of his shorts.

She blinked as he straightened his legs and popped back onto the floor. Luke rolled his shoulders, reached for the towel, and turned. Energy radiated from him as his eyes met hers. A slow, sexy grin spread across his gorgeous face.

Grace's knees buckled.

'Hey. How long have you been there?'

'Um …' How did she speak? She couldn't remember. Words wouldn't form in her brain. 'I … I don't …'

Luke stalked towards her and captured her mouth with his. Her lips parted and his tongue dipped gently into her stunned mouth. Hot and flushed, she shivered. He smelled of sweat and man. She'd have moaned if she hadn't lost use of her vocal cords.

He drew away with a wicked gleam in his eyes. 'You okay?'

Summoning the energy to respond, Grace mentally shook herself. His skin was practically throbbing as the veins in his arms popped and sweat dampened the scatter of dark curls between his pecs. 'Yeah. I just … dammit, Luke. You're so bloody sexy.'

Grinning, his hand pressed to her weak spine as he

brushed his lips against hers. Softly, gently. She groaned, wanting more. Needing more. Her belly coiled tight.

'I still have deadlifts, then I'll be done.' Taking her hand, he led her to a seat. Grace sank into it easily thanks to legs that were no longer working. 'You sit there. I'll be with you in a minute.'

She made some sound of agreement. Luke tossed the towel onto the table and moved over to a barbell he'd set up with a ridiculous amount of weight. She didn't have the brain capacity to count it even if she could see the weight of the bells. Instead, the torture continued as every muscle in Luke's body from head to toe rippled and contracted through his deadlifts. His abs popped until there were twenty of them, the V leading into his shorts never more distinctive. Grace couldn't tear her gaze away.

She found her voice after the first set. 'Um ... how heavy is that?'

Luke guzzled from his water bottle and shrugged. 'One-forty.'

One hundred and forty kilos. Shit. 'That's ... like ... almost three of me.'

He grinned. 'I could probably biceps curl you.'

She could imagine it. 'Damn ... just hurry up already.'

'Why?' Squatting, he set himself up again, planting his feet and wrapping his hands around the bar. 'You want something, babe?'

'No. Yes. Dammit, Luke, I want you.'

His gaze lifted back to hers, 'I know you do' flashing through his azure eyes. 'In a minute.'

The minute turned out to be another four or five incredibly long, torturous, and erotic ones. Now that the shock of him working out had worn off, her thoughts had returned, and they were dirty. Heated blood swirled between her legs. Uncomfortable, she tried crossing them, but it didn't help. She'd always appreciated a fine body and Luke's was far better than fine. He wasn't ridiculously muscled like body builders, but he certainly gave a good Thor impression.

After his last deadlift, he strode towards her and placed his hands on either arm of her plastic chair, grinning as he leaned in close. 'Let me run to warm down and then …' He captured her mouth, slipping his tongue between her lips and leaving her with a promise. 'I'll do you.'

Her toes curled inside her shoes as a breath escaped her lips. Still grinning, Luke hopped on the treadmill, hit a couple of buttons, and started running.

'How was work today?' he asked. 'Something hold you up?'

'Yeah.' She cleared her throat. Work seemed like a million years ago now. 'A kid came off his skateboard and sliced his arm open, down to the bone and everything. Poor thing. Took a while to clean out the wound and Joanne had to do some good suturing, but he'll be all right.'

'That's what this scar on my shin's from, skateboarding as a kid. It was just a cut though, no stitches or anything.'

'Yeah, he was unlucky, but thankfully wearing a helmet. How was your day?'

'I secured a supplier contract with a seafood place in Cairns for fish and prawns, and Bill's on board with the new menu.'

Grace tore her gaze from his iron calves and grinned. 'That's great!'

'Sure is. I'll be busy finalising everything this week. But other than that, Mum called to say she and Dad will be home on the weekend and I had a few chats with the regulars. Old Pete suggested I find myself a nice girl.'

'Yeah?'

'Yeah. Told him I already had one. He said so I should. That was it.'

Warmth enveloped her heart and her belly fluttered. 'Well, I don't know about nice. Right now, I'm feeling incredibly naughty.'

Luke grinned. 'Need to flush these toxins out, babe, else I won't be able to move tomorrow.'

'Yes, I know. How long do you plan to run for?'

'I'd usually go until I was tired, but today I'll do the minimum twenty. Then we can be naughty.'

Grace squeezed her knees together. 'Well, I'm ready.'

After twenty minutes of idle chatter that seemed to last forever, Luke hit the stop button and leapt off the treadmill. Pushing to her feet, Grace wrapped herself around him, hooked her ankles tight, and pressed her hungry mouth to his. Heat soared inside her as her hands pressed to his sweaty back and he eased the door open to bring them into the cool. Her back hit the wall and his heart pounded aerobically against hers as he nipped at her lips and replenished his oxygen with her own.

Oh, she was glad she'd been late leaving work.

He drew away slowly. 'Let's move this into the shower, Grace. I'm disgustingly sweaty.'

She ran her hands up into his damp hair. 'I sort of like it.' She dropped a kiss to his shoulder, his skin hot and salty beneath her tongue as he carried her into the bathroom.

Luke lowered Grace to her feet and made quick work of unbuttoning her red work shirt as she kicked off her shoes. Reaching into the shower, he worked the taps while toeing off his own runners. Grace slipped out of her pants, her underwear, then pressed herself against his back as she slid her fingers into the waistband of his shorts and tugged them down.

Luke turned and pulled her into the cubicle. The lukewarm water did nothing to douse her desire as she curved her body against the rigid planes of his and gazed up into his hooded blue eyes. His hands slid down to cup her butt as hers rested over his glorious chest. Hair stuck to their foreheads as the water warmed and he swooped down to kiss her. She lifted her leg and brushed her knee against his hip, but Luke made no move to satisfy her needs.

'Luke—'

'We need to wash, Grace.' He pulled away and reached for the soap, rubbing it between his hands until froth lathed his fingers. His lips quirked and she stamped her foot back to the tiles.

'I thought we were going to have hot, naughty sex.'

'We will,' he chuckled. 'But first I need to warm you up.'

'Oh, I'm warm.'

He dropped the soap into the holder and brushed his lips against her shoulder. 'Of course you are. But still …'

His soapy hands cupped her breasts, massaging gently. Grace's breath escaped as she gripped his shoulders. His hands brushed over her ribs and belly, then he re-soaped before slipping gently between her legs. Her knees buckled, pulse pounded as his fingers slipped and rubbed. She bit down on her lower lip.

'You want to torture me.'

He chuckled again and kissed her neck. 'Well, we aren't playing a game of "nice".' His hands slipped down her thighs. 'Lift your leg, baby.'

She did, one at a time, her grip hardening around his

shoulders until he announced her clean. Then he took the cake of soap and ran it down his arm.

'Oh, no you don't!' Grace snatched for it and the soap slipped out of his hands before clattering to the floor. 'What about my turn?'

She might want to hurry this up, but she also wanted to run her hands over every inch of his ripped body.

Luke held up his hands in surrender and grinned. 'Sorry. Go ahead.'

She picked up the soap and built up a lather before gripping his shoulder and running her hands down his muscular arm. Her two hands didn't even wrap around his biceps. Shivering, she did the other, then splayed her fingers over his hard pectorals. Goddamn, there was a lot of him. She teased his dark nipples and grinned as his abs rippled beneath her fingers. Then she made him turn so she could do his back, and her heart swooned. Grace had decided during anatomy class that a man's back often went underappreciated. She ran her hands down his sculpted traps, along his spine, and over his terrific lats, every one of them hard and clearly defined. She couldn't wait to see how such a hunk of muscle would suffer at yoga on Thursday.

Running her hands over his butt, she smiled and placed a kiss against his spine. 'You can turn around now.'

When he did, she took him in her soapy hand, and Luke groaned. Grinning, Grace continued to wash him, taking her sweet time as she revelled in returning the torture he'd bestowed upon her. But once she placed the soap back in the holder, there was no holding back. Luke lifted her off her feet and Grace squeezed her legs around his waist as she crushed her mouth to his. Dripping wet, he swept her out of the shower. Grace didn't even know if he turned it off. She didn't care. A moment later, her wet body hit the mattress and Luke quickly prepared himself before returning to kneel over her. His hand gripped her hip as he nibbled at her ear.

'How naughty do you want to be, Grace?'

Her heart leapt and before she could think, she pressed her hand to his chest and urged him back a touch. 'Not very. I'm not into games or props, Luke.' Then she lifted her leg and hooked her knee over his shoulder. 'But I know some excellent positions.'

Chapter Sixteen

Grace's legs continued to shake throughout dinner. A late dinner, it so happened, as she and Luke hadn't been able to get enough of each other, and Grace had loved every second. She wasn't usually so brazen, but Luke made her feel more than any man ever had and she wouldn't apologise for it. Her toes continued to curl against the tiles as she enjoyed her vegetable stir-fry and spring rolls. They'd just finished loading the dishwasher when her phone rang. Leaning her hip on the bench, she picked it up, and her cloud of euphoria dissipated.

'Ergh. It's my dad.' She stared at her phone, nibbling on her lower lip.

'Are you going to answer it?'

She didn't want to. He wouldn't have anything nice to say.

'If I don't, he'll only keep ringing.' And she didn't need that. Taking a deep breath, Grace answered and moved a few steps away. 'Hey, Dad.'

'I hear you're seeing someone.'

She stilled. No 'hello'. No 'how are you'. Just straight to the point with venom in his tone. Heart pounding, she shot her gaze over her shoulder. 'Where did you hear that?'

'Don't deny it, girl. I know what goes on around here. I asked Matt to visit you for New Year's, but he doesn't see the point now that you told him you're fucking someone else. Good job, Grace. You've ruined everything.'

Grace hurried across the room and slid open the back door. She didn't dare look at Luke, who was still pottering about the kitchen. Stepping out into the warm night, she stared into the small backyard and breathed to soften her simmering anger.

'I haven't ruined anything. I told you I wasn't interested in Matt. Not that it's any of your business, but I gave him a shot.'

'You fed a root rat,' Edward spat, and Grace's mouth dropped open. 'He won't come back for seconds if you're spreading it around.'

'Dad!' Grace blinked, her stomach roiling. Words failed her.

'And what you do is my business, young lady. I'm your father and I want what's best for you.'

No, you don't! she wanted to scream, but she bit her tongue. She could barely keep the tremor from her voice as she said, 'Look, I don't know what you're after, and I'm certain there's something you want from the Clarks that you're willing to trade me for, but you need to forget about it. I am *not* "fucking someone" as you so elegantly put it. But I *am* dating, and I don't need my father interfering, so get the hell out of my life!'

The words shrilled from her chest before she could stop them, but despite her hammering heart, a glimmer of pride rose in her belly.

'Grace, do you realise what you have done?' Edward roared.

She didn't bother to keep her voice down. 'I don't care! None of it affects me! I'm sorry that whatever scheme you've tried to pull has failed, but next time, don't use me in it! You and Grandpa screwed up the station and you're going to have to put it back together yourself. I simply do not give a shit.'

Edward's voice hardened. 'Tell me who you're seeing.'

She laughed and rolled her eyes to the dark summer sky. 'Piss off.'

Hands shaking, Grace hung up and blew out a deep belly breath. He might know that she was dating, and she'd worry about that later, but dammit, she hated that he spoke to her like that. Hated that his vile words crawled under her skin and made her feel dirty.

Squeezing her eyes closed, she shook her head. No. She wouldn't let his disgusting comments hurt her. She was not cheap or easy. What she had with Luke was special. Fun. Intimate. And as she slipped back inside the cool house and saw him on the lounge illuminated by the Christmas tree and TV, Grace knew without a doubt that he meant something to her.

Placing her phone on the bench, she crossed the room. He lifted his arm to welcome her as she settled beside him and rested her head on his shoulder. His lips brushed through her hair as she stared at the TV. A reality police show was on, showing a New South Wales copper stepping out of his car on the highway.

'You okay?' Luke asked after a moment.

'Hmm-mmm.' She mindlessly watched the copper and the fuzzy-faced assailant he'd pulled over until her sorrows rose and spilled from her chest. 'My father's an arsehole.'

'Yeah?'

'Yeah.'

'What did he do?'

'I'm never good enough. Not that I care anymore. I gave

up on trying to win his love years ago. He thinks my yoga is stupid and calls me a "bloody vegan" just because I refuse to eat the cows he tortures. The least he could do is use anaesthetic when recommended, but he doesn't because it's too expensive and some other things …' She shuddered, not wanting to think about it as Luke's hand stroked up and down her arm. 'But he treats me like trash and refuses to listen or care about what I want. You know he didn't come to my university graduation?'

'Really?'

'Nope. And not because he couldn't, but he told me, to my face, that he didn't want to. Reckons I didn't need to go to uni.' Drawing in a breath, she released it slowly. 'He broke my heart that day.'

Luke's hand stopped brushing her skin as he drew her into a tighter hold. He dropped another kiss to her hair. 'I'm sorry, Grace.'

She shook her head and focused on the copper. 'It doesn't matter. Mum came and I enjoyed the day. Dad's just an arsehole.' She wouldn't tell him about the way Edward spoke to her. She couldn't.

'I knew you weren't close to your family and Jess always said your father was mean to you. I certainly wouldn't call him friendly, and he's often rude at the pub.'

Her mouth twisted. 'I'm sorry. But yes, he's not nice and he takes no responsibility for anything. He won't accept that the struggle with White Peaks is his fault and he tries all these weird and wonderful schemes to get out of trouble. But it doesn't work 'cause he's been struggling for years.'

'Since well before you or I were born.'

'Exactly! He should have diversified when everyone else did. Tropic Sun, Kelly Station, and Shadow Creek got rid of their cattle and are booming with diversity. I know Tropic Sun struggled for a while there, but they pulled through. Bernie has done well with the coffee plantation and Shadow Creek is rocking it.'

'Yeah. I don't see your dad giving up cattle.'

'It's all he knows. But I don't understand what goes through his head sometimes. He's all about connections and what favours he can get. I don't believe it was an accident that the Hall sisters ended up on Tropic Sun and White Peaks. I mean, I'm sure Zoe and Charlie love each other, but I don't get what she sees in him.' Exhaling, Grace shook her head. 'If only Dad would take personal responsibility for his struggles rather than believe the world owed him something, then he might actually get White Peaks back on track. But he never will because he's a lying, manipulative cheater and probably can't help it 'cause it was bred into him.'

'Yeah … your grandfather was—'

'A thief. A liar.' A man Grace was grateful she'd never met.

'Thankfully, I think those traits skipped your generation.'

Grace smiled and glanced up at him. 'I do my best.'

His eyes gleamed as he stroked her cheek, and the tension around her heart eased. 'You're nothing like your parents, Grace.'

She melted against him. 'Thank you. Because even though it's what my father wants for me, I don't like the idea of being a lying, manipulative, cheating, acre-chaser. If there's one thing I don't want, it's land.'

Luke's eyebrows quirked. 'You don't like the land?'

'Not really. Mum and Dad treated me like a girl and I didn't learn half the stuff Charlie did. Besides, I'm fascinated by medicine and love my work, so I no longer care I never learned how to run a farm.'

'I think being a nurse and teaching yoga suits you.' His arm squeezed her tight. 'And I also think it's time for dessert.'

She smiled and lifted herself away from him. 'Dessert sounds great. What do we have?'

'Would you like a banana split?'

Grace grinned. 'I'd love one.'

They made banana splits with a touch of ice cream, a drizzle of maple syrup, and lots of berries. Luke fed her a strawberry and followed it up with a swift kiss that left her giggling. Everything was so easy with him. He made her feel special. Cherished. She wanted them to remain this way forever.

But as they flipped through the channels until they found the beginning of a *The Big Bang Theory* rerun, worry pooled in Grace's belly. Edward would be onto her now. He was clearly still hung up on the idea of her and Matt, so how long would it take for her father to discover she was with Luke?

She shivered and dug into her banana split. It wouldn't take him long at all.

Chapter Seventeen

'Stop worrying, Grace,' Jessica said as she rolled out a yoga mat. 'You've had many responses to your Facebook event. People will come.'

Claire placed her hand on Grace's shoulder. 'I encouraged everyone who's been in the salon these past few weeks. And with it being the holidays and all, nearly everyone in town has passed through.'

Exhaling, Grace nodded as she continued to twist her fingers together. She knew she shouldn't worry. She'd had wonderful feedback and promises from many people that they'd attend. But she also knew that when it came to the crunch, people often backed out.

'I just want this to be a success.'

'And it will be!' Jessica flung her arm around Grace. 'You'll do a wonderful job and even if half of today's attendees return, you'll be off to a great start.'

'That's true.'

Besides, she hadn't only decided to do this last week. She'd been teaching yoga in Mareeba for years and had developed a business model suitable for her local clientele. She would offer her multiclass cards at a discounted rate today to encourage people to return, and she had an email newsletter for locals to sign up for. But word of mouth worked best and Elizadale thrived on gossip, so all it would take was one person to love her class and others would come in droves.

That one person was the first to arrive.

'Good evening, ladies!' Meg Riley bounced into the hall with a pink yoga mat tucked under her arm. Isabella Brennan followed her.

'Hi, Meg. Isabella. Thank you for coming,' Grace said.

Meg scribbled her name on the sign-in sheet. 'I'm so excited you're doing this, Grace. I'd have gone to one of your classes in Mareeba, but it's just such a drive.'

'It is, which is why I wanted to save myself the trip too. I've been meaning to get this off the ground because yoga can benefit so many people.'

'It's great for the soul, and we all need that sometimes.'

Isabella nodded mutely.

'Well, today's class will involve a mix of everything. We'll do a bit of deep breathing, stretching, strength, and relaxation.'

Meg grinned. 'Sounds excellent. Come on, Iz. Let's grab ourselves a spot at the front.'

Elizadale's crowning jewel skipped away with Isabella as Grace greeted Jenna and Holly from the pharmacy. Emma showed up with her mum, Linda, and the school principal, Deborah Maguire. Elanora Campbell arrived with her mother, Liz Kelly, followed by Sue and Heather. Soon, Grace's spine relaxed and her nerves morphed into excitement as she directed more people to sign in and had never-ending discussions about 'this is a great idea' and 'I hope this helps with my back pain'.

'I'll circulate through the room,' Grace promised Vivian, the aging schoolteacher. 'So if you need any alternatives or look uncomfortable, I'll help you.'

'Thank you, dear.' Vivian smiled and went to find herself a spot. The door opened again to the sound of disgruntled bickering and Grace's heart swelled as Luke ushered in three of his junior teammates.

'I'm so going to pull a hammy.'

'I just hope I don't pull my groin.'

'Ah, shit. Smithy!' The first bloke glared at Luke. 'You owe me, man!'

'He owes you nothing, Gordo,' Joe said, entering behind the team as Luke closed the door. 'We're being supportive community members. Hello, Grace.'

Joe Cooper, the physical education teacher and football team captain, smiled at her and picked up the pen.

'Hi, Joe. Thanks for coming. And for bringing people.'

'We're under duress,' Gordo said politely, a twinkle of cheek in his eye as he took the pen from Joe. 'Though it can't be too hard to stretch for an hour. Or act like a tree. Is that what we're going to do? These ones?'

The young bloke who couldn't be much older than nineteen stuck his foot against his knee and demonstrated an awfully wobbly tree pose. Grace laughed as his mate elbowed him in the ribs.

'Need more practice, Gordo.'

'We could do tree pose,' Grace said, although it hadn't been part of her plan today. 'Maybe next time though, as it's not as easy as you think.'

'Ah, this is how she ropes us back in,' Gordo said, handing the pen to Luke.

Grace smiled. 'Well, it's not possible to do all poses in one class. But thank you for coming.'

'Smithy made us.'

'Call it pre-season training,' Luke said with a smirk.

Gordo rolled his eyes. 'I'd rather do a hundred burpees.'

'We'll do that later,' Joe said. 'But first, let's work on our static and core strength.'

Enjoying the good humoured banter, Grace glanced at the young footy players. 'Well, I hope you enjoy yourselves and I'm grateful for your support. Now, any injuries I need to know about?'

They shook their heads. As Joe and the guys found a spot, Luke stepped up beside Grace and placed his hand on her shoulder. Her heart leapt, but she resisted the urge to sink against him.

'Wow, Grace. Look at the turnout.'

'Over twenty people have arrived and we still don't start for five minutes. Even if half of them return, I'll be happy.'

'It'll grow, I'm sure.'

She smiled up at him. 'Thanks, Luke.'

He joined his friends and after a few more minutes, Grace strode to the front of the room and stood on her mat to face the class. She thanked them all for coming, shared what tonight's class would entail and gave her usual safety spiel about doing things at your own level and how she'd offer alternatives. But since no one came to hear her speak, she encouraged everyone to lie down, close their eyes, and began guiding them through breathing exercises. Grace had turned off the lights and as she made her way through the room of people lying comfortably on their mats, some flat on their backs while others had taken her suggestion of placing a towel beneath their heads or knees, everything inside her softened. She was in her element. She loved nursing, but yoga brought peace unlike anything she could describe and finally, she was sharing that love with everyone lying around her.

'If you want to take it further, breathe deeper, in for three, hold for three, out for three,' she said as she crept quietly between the rows. Some people looked more focused than others, such as Meg and her mum Sue. Others could barely lie still, like Gordo.

Grace paced slowly towards the men trying to hide in the back corner. 'Just focus on the breath. Feel your belly expand, then your ribs, then your chest. Then breathe out through your belly. Your ribs. Your chest deflates last.'

Stopping beside Luke, Grace pressed her lips together. He lay spreadeagled, muscles loose as his flat belly lifted and chest expanded. Then his belly concaved. Pecs deflated. Her own chest expanded as she smiled softly to herself. She might have been hesitant about dating and hated that she feared it, but here was a man lying on a yoga mat far too small for him and focusing on his breath just to support her. Who had brought his friends and didn't care what anyone thought. Heat curled inside her as her hormones did a little dance. What had she done to be so lucky?

Sensing her beside him, Luke peeked his eyes open. Her heart lurched as he smiled softly and winked. Grace's grin was a reflex. Then he closed his eyes again. Taking a deep breath herself, she refocused and moved on.

'All right. Let go of the breath and resume normal breathing. Slowly bring one knee into your chest, then the other, and hug them close.'

The rest of the class ran smoothly as she guided everyone

through abdominal work, then moved onto standing poses. Before Grace knew it, night had fallen and she was dimming the lights for savasana. She gave them five minutes, then joined everyone in a cross-legged position as she pressed her hands together beneath her chin.

'Namaste.'

A murmur rippled through the room, followed by cheerful chatter as everyone rolled up the mats. Feeling lighter than air, Grace pushed herself to her feet. She'd done it. And as she moved towards the door, Grace found herself inundated with gratitude.

'You can count me in for every Thursday,' Meg said.

'Me too,' Elanora agreed. 'I enjoyed that, Grace. It'll be a great way to manage my stress levels.'

'Absolutely,' Isabella agreed. 'I'll be here every week.'

Grinning, Grace thanked the ladies and as they approached Jessica to purchase multiclass passes, she turned to chat to more people and revelled in her success.

* * *

Only mildly surprised at how much he'd enjoyed the session, Luke drove Grace away from the community centre. His body felt lighter, relaxed, and even though he was sure parts of him would ache tomorrow, it had been worth it to witness the delight in Grace's eyes.

They had to celebrate that.

'I thought we could go to the roadhouse for dinner,' he suggested as he drove down Riley Road. He felt rather than saw Grace hesitate as he indicated to turn onto the highway. 'Is that all right?'

He glanced her way and while a cloud shaded her gaze, he

relaxed at her serene smile. 'Dinner sounds great, Luke. Let's hope Samantha is running a good special.'

'She usually does.' The roadhouse's fabulous cook, Samantha Hudson, often ran specials that ranged from pizza to Chinese to anything else that wasn't regularly sold in town. 'Then afterwards, I thought maybe we could walk around town and check out the Christmas lights?'

'I'd like that. I've seen some, but I haven't driven past the acreage lots yet.'

They arrived at the roadhouse and Luke's stomach rumbled as they climbed out of his ute. Samantha might not have the professional qualifications of a chef, but she was a fantastic cook and as they strode into the restaurant, both Luke and Grace were happy to discover that Thai was on the menu tonight. Locals gathered around tables nibbling on spring rolls and wrapping noodles around forks. He'd been worried that Grace might not be ready to be seen together in public, but she seemed completely unperturbed as they ordered and sat at a table by the window.

Smiling softly to himself, he dug into the Pad Thai. 'I'm pleased you had a great turnout tonight, Grace.'

Her eyes sparkled as she bit into a chicken skewer. 'I still can't believe it.'

'We live in a supportive community,' he reminded her.

'We do. And you did rather well too.'

He chuckled. 'Yeah, I saw you checking me out.'

'I was observing your technique.'

'Tell yourself that all you want. But I'll admit, I enjoyed it.'

She beamed. 'Maybe we can do yoga more often. Just the two of us.'

Luke pressed his lips together as he thought about the 'yoga' they'd done the other night. In bed. And even though he knew that wasn't what she was referring to, he could see the benefits regular practice would have for both of them. 'We can do that. Especially considering I won't be able to attend classes since Jessica's already taken those nights off work.'

They finished their dinner, then drove back to his house for their walk. Luke switched on his Christmas tree lights and left it sparkling festively in the window as he and Grace strolled down Abbott Street, chatting idly. Luke simply enjoyed being out with her, despite the warm evening. Arriving at Riley Road, they wandered up to view the large Christmas tree outside Riley House, the historic Queenslander that dated back to the time of settlement and now operated as the Town Centre.

'I love how festive Elizadale gets,' Grace said as they gazed up at the tree. The sparkling star on top sat level with the roof while massive red and gold baubles decorated the fake pine needles.

'Small communities are the best at such things.'

Once they finished admiring Riley House, Luke led Grace down Elizabeth Street towards Margaret Riley's. Her Christmas light display had always been the best, which wasn't surprising when she'd spent the last fifty-odd years decorating the same beautiful house. Lights and decorations covered every inch of the house and, like always, she stood at the fence chatting to the admirers and serving biscuits. She might be in her seventies, but nothing slowed Elizadale's matriarch down.

'Merry Christmas!' she called when she spotted them.

'Merry Christmas, Mrs Riley,' Luke replied.

'My, my, Luke Smithfield hand in hand with Grace White.' She smiled as they stopped by her fence, her eyes twinkling. 'This is new.'

Luke squeezed Grace's hand. 'Very. How are you, Mrs Riley?'

'Wonderful, my lad. Would you two like a biscuit?'

Typically, she'd cut them in shapes of Christmas characters. Luke selected a chocolate snowman while Grace chose Santa.

She leaned her head on Luke's shoulder as she bit into the biscuit, and his heart swelled with more than Christmas cheer.

After a moment, they looped back to Jackson Villas, which Luke had yet to see. Grace, her friends, and neighbours had done a fantastic job, the four units decorated festively while unit five sat dark and vacant.

Walking up to the top end of Station Drive, they started along the winding path running alongside Shadow Creek. The farm may no longer be a cattle station, but the street name remained. Luke watched Grace, smiling softly as her hair blew in the breeze.

'What do you want for Christmas, Grace?'

She tore her gaze from the candy canes decorating Shadow Creek's entrance and raised her eyebrows. 'You don't need to get me anything.'

'But what if I want to? Do you like candles? Decorative knickknacks? Sparkling jewellery?'

Her eyes glittered. 'I'm a typical girl, Luke. I like anything pretty. But honestly, I've never been into the whole gift-giving thing. My family weren't good at it.'

'Well, my family is. And seeing as how you helped me with the menu and have spent time in my bed, I need to get you something.'

He wrapped his arm around her waist as an adorable blush pinked her cheeks. 'That means I'll need to get you something.'

'No, it doesn't. You've given me enough.'

'But you can't buy me a gift and then tell me that—' She froze, her feet rooting to the spot as she watched a white ute drive past.

Luke frowned, following her gaze as the car turned around the corner. 'What is it?'

'It's …' Her breath hitched and alarm filled her eyes, but she shook her head and it disappeared. 'Nothing. Just my brother Charlie.'

Grace let out a deep breath as Luke turned to where Charlie's taillights had disappeared. 'All right …'

He didn't get a chance to formulate a question though as Grace tugged at his hand. 'Come on, let's keep going. We'll look at Meg's lights and then we need to see the acreage lots.'

But Luke could hardly take in the lights, distracted by Grace's reaction to her brother as they strolled past the magnificent country homes on acreage at the southern end of town. Had that been fear in her eyes? Why would the sight of Charlie cause her to freeze like that?

Admiring Ron and Sue Riley's house, a true fiesta of spirit, Luke held Grace in his arms and breathed in her strawberry scented hair. He couldn't blame her if she was afraid. Her issues with her family weren't minor and her pain had been apparent when she'd spoken of her father's disappointment. What kind of man didn't attend his daughter's university graduation? It was disgusting and he could see now just how much it had damaged her.

A cold wave shuddered through him. Was that why she wanted to keep them a secret? Was she afraid that Charlie having seen them would burst the protective bubble she'd placed around their relationship?

Shit. Of course. She was nervous about dating and he

didn't need to be a genius to figure out why. It wasn't an uncommon story. A woman hurt by her father could easily develop trust issues.

But he cared about her. She was becoming the most important person in the world to him. So, furious with Edward, Luke held Grace close and pressed a kiss to her soft hair. And vowed that he'd keep her safe.

Chapter Eighteen

Grace spent the next two days preparing for a fight. Charlie had undoubtedly seen her and Luke out in each other's arms. Eventually, he would tell their father and Edward would pounce at the opportunity to call and abuse her.

So why hadn't he? She was ready. The confrontation might have scared her at first, but going out in public with Luke had been a risk she'd been willing to take. She couldn't sacrifice what they were building by insisting on keeping their relationship a secret. Grace had to stand up to her father. She'd fought him on her career, living situation, yoga, and she would fight him on this too. Her father might be a manipulative old bastard who wanted to control her, but she was a strong, independent woman and wasn't afraid of her daddy. Let him sabotage her and Luke all he liked. Edward couldn't break them.

At least that's what Grace told herself, but deep down, she couldn't stop shaking.

On Saturday afternoon, she and her friends arrived at the Elizadale Christmas Fair. The church always did a good job by putting on the nativity display and allowing locals to sell their crafts. Claire had created beautiful hairclips for adults and children, some plain and pretty, while others sported logos or pictures that would appeal to the kids. Grace particularly liked the Disney ones and knew they would sell quickly as she arranged them on the table.

'They look great, Claire. Mums will buy plenty for their little girls.'

'I hope so.' Claire sat in her plastic chair behind the table and crossed her long legs. 'Do you two want first dibs?'

Jessica bought two scrunchies and a Cowboys hair clip, which made Grace think of Luke. Pity he wouldn't like a Cowboys hair clip because she had to get him something and the fair tonight was her best chance.

She selected a colourful scrunchie for herself and tied it into her ponytail, then left with Jessica to browse the stalls spread out on the lawn at the golf course.

'I need to buy some of Rebecca's candles, then get a slice or something from Lucy Maguire 'cause I'm starving. Is there anything you need, Grace?'

'I'll pick up a thing or two, but I've done most of my shopping.'

Arriving at the soap stall, they bought a few bars for their respective mothers and themselves. Then they stopped by Lucy Maguire's baking stall and purchased gift bags of coconut slice and rumballs. Jessica spent a small fortune on Rebecca Taylor's candles and they stocked up on a few doilies from little old Mrs Thompson.

At the jam and chutney stall, Grace randomly selected a small jar for her father, a bigger one for Charlie, then took more care in choosing one for Luke. Next time they made pancakes, they could enjoy them with delicious homemade rosella jam.

They were running out of stalls, though, and she didn't know what else to buy Luke. She couldn't just give him food. Why did it seem like the markets were targeted more towards women?

Maybe she'd stop by the homewares store and find something there. Not that she knew what she was looking for. She was terrible at buying gifts. Like she'd told Luke, it wasn't something her family did well. Her parents had always bought her what she needed, including new school shoes and learners plates the Christmas before she turned sixteen. Sure, she would receive a book she'd asked for and maybe some pretty bath products or makeup, but her mother had rarely put any thought into the gifts. It was Jessica who'd shown Grace the creativity behind gift giving with the landscapes she painted her loved ones and the photo gifts she arranged. These days, Grace had no trouble showing her friends how much they meant to her. But Luke?

She was stumped.

* * *

Heart pounding, Luke watched as his father scratched his head and read the new menu. His parents had returned home late last night and this morning, Luke hadn't wasted a second when his father had asked for an update. He'd mentioned his desire to change the menu months ago, so Nick Smithfield showed no surprise when Luke had proudly presented him with his idea.

'It's certainly different,' his father said, eyebrows raising.

'But not too different. Right? I mean, it has all the family favourites.'

'I like the new fish dishes. Barra sells well.'

'And I've sourced some good barra from a farm near Cairns. It's as local as I can get.'

'Excellent.' Nick placed the menu down and met Luke's gaze across the desk. 'Then I don't know why you're looking for my approval. You better get your butt into gear if you're launching on New Year's Eve.'

Luke grinned, joy bursting from his chest as though he was a kid again. No matter how old you got, it seemed you never wanted to stop pleasing your parents. 'Thank you, Dad. Bill and I have it all sorted and are ready to go. But even though you gave me free rein to manage the pub as I like, I'm grateful for the support.'

Luke followed his father to his feet, meeting him in a handshake before Nick wrapped his arm around his shoulders. 'You know you'll always have it.'

He did, and it was something he'd taken for granted. His parents would always be there for him and support his dreams. They'd allowed him to play every sport he wished and had driven him all over the Tablelands and North Queensland in his youth to attend games and sporting carnivals. They'd never batted an eye when he'd taken off to work around the country. Their support was something he'd relied on. Treasured. Something he thought all parents did. Until he'd got to know Grace.

Her strength and compassion sure were a testament to her resilience.

'Now,' Nick said, grabbing the menu off the desk. 'Tell me more about the changes. Have we dropped any suppliers?'

Luke updated his father on where he'd sourced new stock and the alterations he'd made with their regular supply order. He and Bill had spent all week working on it, and the streamlined process had left Luke impressed. The menu was exactly what he'd wanted with lean, rich food ranging from nachos to stir-fry to roast of the day. They'd serve juicy steaks, grilled mackerel, and baked salmon. He'd redesigned the steak sandwich and chicken burger to sit alongside the pumpkin burger. He had three delicious salads that weren't the traditional garden variety and starters that made his mouth water.

Most importantly, nothing was deep fried. The commercial air fryers would arrive tomorrow and everything was in position to launch on time for the New Year Extravaganza.

On Friday night, he'd put out a sign announcing the upcoming change. But while he'd received the expected apprehension and complaints from customers, curiosity had won out.

'I don't think I've seen Mum so excited in a while,' Jessica said as she wiped over the liquor bottles on Tuesday afternoon. 'And you've certainly pulled it together quickly. Not that I'm surprised.'

Luke smiled as he unloaded the dishwasher. 'There's no point holding back when you want something, Jess. And it's certainly sent a buzz around town.'

'Yeah, I've heard about your new menu,' John Taylor said from the other side of the bar where he sat with his son, Jason, nursing a beer. 'Sounds interesting. We'll be in town on New Year's, so we'll definitely have dinner here.'

'Thanks, John,' Luke said. 'You won't be sorry. And the grandkids should love the new kids menu too.'

'Dunno how when you're getting rid of the chips,' Ben mumbled from further down the bar. 'What good's a pub with no chips? The kids won't like it.'

Luke ignored the twinge in his chest as he offered the older man a small smile. Ben was a loyal customer and had a chicken parma and chips at the Smithfield every Monday night. Had done so for years. It was the customers like Ben that Luke had been worried about, but it was a risk he'd been willing to take to achieve this dream.

'Kids don't need chips,' he replied politely. 'We want a fresher image, Ben. And to serve nice food. Maybe you'll like our sweet potato wedges.'

Ben grunted. 'Have you at least kept the steaks with garlic butter?'

'Of course.' He'd changed it to garlic nut-butter, but Ben didn't need to know that.

'Might find something new to eat then,' he muttered. 'But don't think I won't be getting my parmy at the Royal, Smithfield. A man needs these little things in life.'

Luke nodded as he loaded another tray into the dishwasher. 'You're welcome to your parmy, Ben, but I hope you find a new favourite on this menu. There's some delicious food on there.'

John smiled. 'Claire said something about pineapple rice.' John Taylor was Claire's father.

'Pineapple rice!' Ben cried, his mouth twisting. 'Shit, man. That's worse than pineapple on pizza.'

'What's wrong with pineapple on pizza?' Jason asked, chuckling as he glanced at Ben. 'Ham and pineapple is a classic.'

'It's *wrong*.'

Luke shook his head. 'I think I might have to agree with Jason on that one. Pineapple makes everything better.'

'Bloody nutters, the lot of you.' Ben took another swig of his beer and Luke turned back to the Taylors.

'The coconut chicken on pineapple rice is one highlight. And I'd strongly recommend the pineapple cheesecake too.'

'Sounds like Rebecca and I will need to have a date night,' Jason said. 'She loves cheesecake.'

'If you're thinking date night, we also have a chocolate fondue for two that you might enjoy.'

Jason grinned. 'I'll lock it in, Smithfield.'

* * *

The tumbler of Bundaberg Rum shattered against the wall. Reddish gold liquid seeped down the stained cream paint as Edward kicked a chair over. It was true. That worthless daughter of his was dating. And rather than enjoy the splendours of what the rich husband he'd picked out for her could provide, she'd moved onto the bloody publican.

Edward gritted his teeth. He wouldn't stand for it. Mary Smithfield was nothing but a nosy bitch who'd had a hand in destroying his happiness. He'd lost his first love because of her and had settled for Francesca. Not that Franny had displeased him, but he would have had another farm if he'd managed to keep that other girl. Except fucking Mary had pulled the best friend card and convinced her to leave him.

Over his dead body would he allow Grace to be with Mary's son. What good was a connection with the local pub? Sure, he liked his grog, but he needed Grace on the land. And he wanted Redback. He needed that station. If Luke Smithfield was in the way, then he'd fix that.

Chapter Nineteen

Luke opened the pub on Christmas Eve, looking forward to the day off tomorrow and the accompanying festivities. Grace was staying over tonight and he couldn't wait to wake up with her on Christmas morning, share breakfast, and exchange gifts before going their separate ways. He wished things were different and that he could spend all day with her, but Christmas breakfast and evening would have to be enough for now. And he planned to spoil her. Grace hadn't been special to many people and he wanted to show her that to him, she was everything. So he'd picked out a few soaps at the church fair he'd thought would complement the aroma of her creamy skin and when he and Joe had visited Cairns yesterday, Luke had popped into the jewellery store as where else would a man go to shop for the woman he loved? Because yes, he loved her. It wasn't a clench of the throat or shock to the heart realisation, but mere acceptance of long brewing feelings. He'd always cared about Grace and had enjoyed every moment he'd spent with her these past few weeks. So even though she'd told him not to, he'd bought her a gift to remind her how much she meant to him, which he hoped to do every Christmas for the rest of his life.

Buoyant, Luke got to work as the usual morning crowd trickled into Smithy's and he engaged in light chatter with the regular blokes. Considering the holidays, the pub wasn't too busy. Single people who had no family came in to socialise and groups of friends sat around tables. It was sad but comforting at the same time as at least these blokes had the pub and each other to spend time with. Not everyone celebrated Christmas with grand family affairs, so Luke was happy to be the one to provide drinks and food for the lonely holiday hearts. He poured beers, talked nonsense, promoted the menu launch, and had just put through an order for a counter meal when Edward White walked through the door.

The older man's gaze locked onto Luke's and his spine stiffened. He wasn't sure why. The man didn't intimidate him. Edward was no better than the lying thief his father had been and as far as Luke was concerned, the only good thing Edward had ever done was bring Grace into this world.

How she'd turned out to be kind and charitable was a mystery.

Edward leaned his elbow on the bar and tipped back his hat. 'I hear you've been fooling around with my daughter.'

Straight to the point, then. Luke placed his hands on the lower side of the bar and looked Edward squarely in the eye. 'We've been dating.'

The disapproval twisting Edward's mouth put Luke's back up. 'You must be some man.'

Not wanting to play this game, Luke didn't reply.

After a moment, Edward's jaw twitched. 'Look, Luke. Grace isn't the girl you think she is.'

Luke's hands tightened over the bar. His biceps flinched, but he remained calm. 'I think I know her well enough.'

Edward barked out a laugh. 'Yeah, right. I bet she drew you in, twisted you around that dirty little finger of hers and slipped you into bed. Don't think I don't know my daughter, Smithfield. She's no better than any other manipulative hussy.'

Teeth clenching, Luke released a slow, steady breath. It took all his strength not to grab the old man by the throat and punch his lights out. 'Don't talk about Grace like that.'

Edward raised his bushy eyebrows. 'You don't agree? Are you sure she didn't turn it on for you?'

'It's none of your business.'

Edward's eyes darkened. 'That girl is my business. And Grace is far from honest, Smithfield. She likes to keep her secrets.'

Secrets? What secrets? Sure, she'd wanted to keep their relationship a secret, but she'd abandoned that notion when she'd happily gone out in public with him. 'There are no secrets between me and Grace.'

Edward scoffed. 'Really?'

'Really. Say whatever you want, White, but our relationship is *not* your business and you have no say in it.'

A wicked gleam filled the old man's eyes as his lips curved. 'Really?'

'Really.'

'What about her fiancé?'

Luke blinked. 'Her what?'

'Her fiancé,' Edward repeated. 'Matt Clark, our neighbour on Redback Station. The man Grace intends to marry.'

Fiancé? Marry? Redback Station? Keeping secrets ...

Luke straightened and stepped away from the bar.

'Yeah.' Edward smirked. 'It's a bit like that. So, you listen to me, Smithfield. I don't want you anywhere near my daughter. Nothing is to come between her and Matt's union. Do you understand?'

Luke's mind fuzzed. 'Or what?'

'Or you might find your own business in trouble.' The old man dipped his chin. 'It's a hard thing to stay successful these days, Smithfield, and you never know what can happen in a pub like this. I'd hate to see your pathetic family lose everything they've worked so hard for.'

Smirking, Edward turned on his heel and strode out of the pub, the door barely slamming him in the arse on the way out.

Luke's heart hammered. His hands tightened on the bar. Grace couldn't be engaged. She'd been hesitant about a relationship because of the pain she'd experienced being raised by her controlling father, not because she'd promised herself to another man. Right?

Shaking his head, Luke marched down to the other end of the bar. Edward White was not a man to be trusted. He had too much of his father in him and old Ian White had died in prison after his theft had altered the farming community in Elizadale forever.

But as Luke gazed about the pub, a chill shot through his body. This place meant everything to him. His parents had built it from scratch. He'd spent his childhood here and planned to work there forever.

Would Edward really try to destroy it?

* * *

After lunch, Grace made her obligatory trip to White Peaks. It was a useless trip when she could have brought her food and presents out tomorrow, but her mother had insisted and Grace didn't want to argue this close to Christmas.

Forcing a smile, she entered the house. 'Hey, Mum!'

Zoe appeared in the kitchen doorway. 'Let me help you,' she said, relieving Grace of the salad and the bag of wine. Zoe, at least, would be pleasant to spend Christmas with.

'Thanks,' Grace said, entering the kitchen where her mother was preparing a feast.

'Hi, Grace. Did you bring the salad?'

'Yep. Pasta.'

Francesca frowned at the container Zoe carried. 'Doesn't look like pasta salad.'

Grace resisted rolling her eyes. 'It's not a covered-in-mayo pasta salad. It's got veggies and a light vinegar dressing.'

Francesca turned back to the chicken she was crumbing. 'Whatever. Put it in the fridge, Zoe.'

Heart sinking, Grace forced cheer into her voice. 'I brought wine! Two bottles.'

'Just two? For all of us?'

Grace let out a slow breath. 'Well, I didn't think I was footing the entire wine bill. I can pick up some more, but I can't pay for it all.'

Francesca tsked. 'I'll give you fifty bucks and you can bring more tomorrow.'

'All right.' Grace moved towards the fridge, slipping the wine inside as her father walked into the kitchen. Her stomach tightened. 'Hi, Dad.'

'Thought you might reject us for Christmas too.'

'Where else do I have to go?' she asked pleasantly, even though she wished she'd had another choice. Luke's family would have appreciated her pasta salad. 'Where's Charlie?'

'Fixing a pipe. Work never stops.'

There was always work to do unless Edward said otherwise. And otherwise didn't include Grace's twenty-first birthday bash. 'I'm going to place these presents under the tree.'

She moved into the lounge room and took her sweet time arranging the gifts. She needed to remain calm. Friendly. She would spend a few minutes helping her mother, then get the hell out of there.

She was measuring ingredients for the apple crumble when her father returned and grabbed a beer from the fridge.

'Stopped by The Smithfield today,' he announced.

Grace's spine stiffened. *Stay calm. Just stay calm.* 'Yeah?'

'You should have told me,' Francesca said lightly. 'You could have got me more wine.'

'Grace can bring some tomorrow. Do you get a discount on grog, girl?'

Grace's hands stilled. Her throat tightened. Heart pounded. Forcing herself to take a breath, she straightened and glanced over her shoulder. Edward leaned casually against the kitchen bench, smugness in his eyes.

She had to play this cool. 'Why would I?'

'You should if you've been spreading your legs for the publican.'

Francesca gasped. 'Edward!'

Grace dusted off her hands, grabbed a tea-towel, and turned to face her father. 'Okay, Dad. You know. Happy now?'

Edward slammed his beer down on the bench, making both Grace and Zoe jump. He took two steps towards Grace. She didn't move.

'Happy? Why would I be happy? I had a perfectly

good man lined up for you, and you turned Matt down for *Luke*?'

Grace threw the tea-towel on the bench with a snap. 'What is wrong with Luke, Dad? How is he any different from Matt? He'll inherit his own property too. Yeah, it's not a cattle station or two or a huge bloody stud, but he does well at Smithy's. Besides, *I* like him, which is more than I can say for Matt Clark.'

'You liked him enough to fuck him!'

'Don't talk to me like that!' Fury surged from her belly up into her chest. Her fists clenched, heart pounded. She would not let him make her feel cheap again, not about Matt *or* Luke. 'I slept with Matt because I wanted to. I'm a grown woman and can do what I like. I don't know what it is you want out of Redback or what deal you made, but you *have* to get over it! You can't *use* me like this! I'm not one of your bloody cows!'

'Oh, please …' Francesca started, but Edward silenced her with an angry hiss.

He pointed a stubby finger at Grace. 'You listen to me, young lady. I won't be talked to that way. I'm your father and you owe me some respect.'

Grace's eyes rolled. '*Pfft*. As if yo—'

A smack rang through the kitchen as Edward's hand collided with her cheek. Grace gasped, stumbling into the bench. Zoe screamed. Some small miracle had Francesca across the kitchen in a flash, pushing Edward away from advancing on Grace again.

Tears welled in Grace's eyes as she lifted a shaking hand to her stinging cheek. Zoe was at her side, asking if she was all right while Francesca yelled at Edward. Grace didn't hear what they were saying as her breath rasped in her throat. Zoe forced a bag of frozen peas against her cheek.

'I don't care what your deal with Matt is, it's no reason to hit your daughter!' Francesca whirled to Grace. 'Honey, are you okay?'

She nodded, struggling for words as she begged herself not to cry. She didn't want to give her father the satisfaction. Taking the peas from Zoe, Grace grabbed the tea-towel and wrapped it around the bag before placing the coolness back to her face. She glared at her father. 'What the hell is wrong with you?'

Edward grabbed his beer. 'You ruined everything. But if you know what's good for you, you'll bloody well fix it.'

'Don't you dare blame me.' Her voice threatened to break as she turned to the ladies. 'Mum, I'm sorry, but I can't stay. I'll come tomorrow to see you, Charlie, and Zoe. But after that, I'm done.'

She handed the peas to her sister-in-law and asked Zoe to finish the apple crumble as she gathered her keys. Grace's heart ached, but she wouldn't cry. Not until she was alone.

'Yeah, run home crying to your boyfriend,' Edward taunted. 'Some tough woman you are.'

Grace didn't reply as she took two steps towards the door.

'But don't expect a warm welcome from him, girl. I told Luke the truth.'

Grace halted. Turning slowly, she glared at Edward, her heart pounding at the triumph in his eyes. 'What did you do?'

He shrugged and lifted his beer for another swig. 'Told him you were engaged to Matt Clark.'

Grace's keys landed with a metallic clatter on the wooden floor as her hand flew to her mouth. She blinked, her stomach roiled, but it wasn't anger she felt. Not rage. It was hate. Unadulterated hate for the man she'd formally thought of as her father.

Zoe gasped while Francesca started yelling again.

'You did what? Edward! How could you?'

'What else was I to do? We need that deal with Redback, Franny. And Grace would be happy with Matt if she damn well tried.' The smugness returned to his eyes as he glanced at Grace. 'Smithfield didn't take it too well. Bloody devastated he was. Called you awful things, so he won't want to see you again.'

Grace didn't think. She ran at her father. 'You bastard!' Tears ran down her cheeks as she pummelled her tiny fists at his chest. 'You evil, sadistic *bastard*!'

Francesca tried to intervene, but she wasn't quick enough. Edward's hands tightened around Grace's arms, squeezing until her bones creaked. She yelped.

'It's for your own good, young lady! If you had any respect for your family, you'd have done as you were bloody well told!'

He shoved her to the floor. Pain shot up her spine as she landed on her backside, her head and shoulder colliding with the cabinet. Grace's vision blurred as hot tears ran down her face. Her heart constricted. She couldn't breathe.

Francesca was shouting again, but Grace tuned them out. Rolling onto her knees, she dropped her head into her hands, unable to stop the tears. Pain filled her chest as her breath escaped in short, sharp bursts.

How could her father be so cruel? Sure, he'd never loved her. Not like a father should. But to destroy her chance of happiness?

Doubling over her knees, her stomach clenched. She'd known he'd do something like this. He'd destroyed any chance of a future with Adam, and now he'd done it again. He'd hurt Luke, intentionally turned him against her, and destroyed their relationship.

Why?

Zoe knelt at her side, placing her hand on Grace's sore shoulder as she provided words of comfort. But they didn't help.

Why would Luke believe him? Why would she be engaged to Matt but dating Luke? Surely, after these past few weeks, Luke wouldn't believe that. What had Edward implied? That Grace had used Luke for a bit of pre-wedding fun?

Dammit, why hadn't she warned Luke?

Grace gripped her knees and tried to regain control. But every time she inhaled, oxygen chugged back out in sobs. Her nails dug into her thighs. She had to find her centre. She couldn't let Edward defeat her. She needed to pull herself up and find Luke. She could fix this. Then she would never see Edward White again.

With another strained breath, Grace straightened and stood, brushing the damp hair off her forehead as she turned to face her father. He continued to lean against the bench, drinking his beer while Francesca sent him a silent glare. Grace couldn't expect much more from her mother.

'Are you done?' Edward asked dryly.

Grace straightened her shoulders. 'Yep. Good job, Dad, you've officially washed your hands of me. Don't think for a *second* that I'm *ever* going to have anything to do with you again! Don't expect me tomorrow, Mum. Merry Christmas, Zoe.

Snatching her keys off the floor, Grace strode out of the house. Her mother called after her, but Grace didn't stop. She started the car and tore away from the homestead, leaving a cloud of dust in her wake.

She wouldn't forgive him. Not this time. Their relationship had been hanging by a thread, and Edward had snapped that.

She had no interest in trying to fix it anymore. Whether or not he'd hurt Luke, he'd hurt her plenty, and she was done.

But she wouldn't let him destroy her relationship with Luke. What they had was special. More than she'd realised. It would break her heart to lose him now.

Chapter Twenty

Grace called Luke when she returned to mobile reception. The phone rang and rang. When he didn't answer, she swore and pressed the button again, trying not to panic. It rang out and she cursed him for not having a message service. She didn't have time to stop and text.

Finally, she slowed into the eighty-kilometre zone, passed the roadhouse, and arrived in town. Luke was working, so she went straight to Smithy's and swung her car into a park out the front.

She ran inside and found Jessica behind the bar. 'Where's Luke?'

'Grace? Oh my God, are you okay?'

'I'm fine.' She must look terrible, though, as Jessica hurried out from behind the bar. 'Where's Luke? Is he here? I need to talk to him.'

'No, he left early. Said something important had come up.'

Groaning, Grace gripped her hair and pulled tight. No, Luke couldn't have believed Edward. He was smarter than that. Surely!

But he didn't know the true nature of her father or how far he would go, so she needed to find him. Turning, Grace ran out of the pub, leaving Jessica calling her name.

She didn't take the car. Heart pounding, she ran the short distance to Luke's house, barely looking as she crossed Jabiru Road. Her sandals smacked along the concrete path and sweat trickled down her back.

Arriving at Luke's, she raced over the grass and skidded to a halt outside his door. Unable to catch her breath, she started banging.

'Luke! Open up! Please!' Tears streamed down her face. 'Luke, listen. It's not—'

The door flew open. 'Grace? What are you doing?'

She stepped back as he pushed open the flyscreen door. Cool air hit her in welcome relief. Luke's expression remained blank, his eyes unreadable.

Then they widened. 'Shit, Grace, what happened to you?'

Grace stared at him. Luke didn't look mad. He didn't seem to hate her. 'My father dropped by the Smithfield earlier …'

'I know.' Jaw tightening, Luke shook his head. 'He's a bastard, Grace. He—'

Grace launched herself at him, burying her face into his chest to smother a fresh wave of sobs. Luke wrapped his arms around her and slammed the wooden door closed.

'I'm so sorry!' She hiccupped, heat rising in her cheeks. She'd acted like a complete fool, but it didn't matter. Everything inside Grace softened until she all but crumbled. Luke hadn't believed Edward.

With an oath, Luke slid his arm behind her back and knees, lifted her up, and carried her to the lounge. 'Grace, baby, you're scaring me. Tell me what happened.'

He sat on the lounge, holding her as he gently lifted her chin. Grace met his gaze as his thumb brushed over her aching cheek. Fire flashed through his eyes.

'Dad told you lies.'

'I know. He came into the pub and—'

She didn't care. Grace kissed him with everything she could muster despite her aches, new tears falling down her cheeks. Her shattered heart swelled and joy burst through her like she'd never felt before. Luke returned her kiss with equal passion, his hand slipping into her hair.

She pulled away first. 'I'm sorry. I'm so sorry.'

Luke's eyebrows shot up. 'What for?'

'I should have warned you about Edward. I should have told you about Matt. There was nothing to tell, but that's what's been going on.'

Grace told Luke everything. How Edward had tried setting her up and that Matt had invited her to Toowoomba. How her refusal had sent Edward into a rage.

'He blames me for ruining some deal he had. I knew there had to be one as he treats me no better than a bloody heifer. Not that it matters because he can't control me, but I knew when he found out about you, he'd try to break us apart. I just never thought … oh, Luke. I'm so sorry.'

She buried her face against his shoulder, hissing at the sting in her cheek. Grace adjusted herself to avoid the pain as Luke's arms tightened around her. Her pulse slowed and tears dried as he danced feathered kisses through her hair.

'No, Grace. I'm sorry. I should have called you after he'd left. But I was busy with … did he tell you about the threat?'

She jerked back. 'No. What did he do?'

'He told me to stay away from you and not get between you and Matt. It sounded like if I didn't, he'd destroy the pub.'

Gasping, Grace tried pushing herself to her feet. 'No! Luke, I won't—'

He didn't release her from his hold. 'Shh, don't worry. I've just got back from the police station.'

Her spine softened. 'Oh. Good.'

'Oh, baby ...' His eyes softened as he wiped her damp face with his thumbs. 'You didn't think I believed him, did you?'

She pressed her lips together. 'He told me you did, but I hoped it wasn't true. I tried calling you and when you didn't answer, I got upset. Then Jessica said you had left because of something important and I panicked.'

Luke's chest heaved as he gripped her chin and brought her gaze to his. 'If I can be frank, and I think I can, I've never liked your father. He's a liar, a cheat, and thinks he can get away with threatening people. But I'm not afraid to stand up to him because you ...' The heat in his eyes softened into smouldering desire. 'Dammit, Grace, you're beautiful. You're sweet, kind, and I love you. I love you so damn much. So why the hell would I listen to a crazed drunk tell me something disgusting about the woman I love? I'll never believe anything, Grace, unless it's from your beautiful lips.'

Melting in his embrace, her heart soared as she hiccupped a smile. Luke loved her. Part of her had suspected that and her own feelings had been growing, but the moment he'd opened that door and she'd realised he hadn't believed her father, she'd found solid ground.

Luke was the one.

Grace blamed her tears on the fact that the floodgates were already open as she wrapped her arms tighter around his neck. She kissed him long and hard, showing him in every way that she felt the same. Then she pulled back, met his warm blue eyes, and grinned. 'I love you too.'

He squeezed his powerful arms around her until she laughed. Luke had faith in her. He hadn't believed Edward. If her father hadn't managed to break them up, then nothing ever could.

'Spend Christmas with me, Grace?'

'Yes.' She placed a smacking kiss on his mouth. 'I will.'

'We'll have breakfast and I have a few gifts for you, then we'll meet my family at church.'

'Your mum won't mind?'

'Mum has prepared a feast, so one extra person won't be a problem.'

'I'll be very grateful.' Grinning, Grace kissed him. 'Thank you, Luke.'

'Always, Grace.' His eyes darkened. 'I should get you some ice for that cheek.'

Her hand lifted to touch. 'Is it bad?'

'Any mark on you is bad.'

'Zoe put ice on it for a minute. It's a little sore, but I'll be all right.'

Luke brushed her hair behind her ear to examine her cheek, his eyes glowering. 'I hate him even more for doing that to you. Do you want to go to the police?'

She raised her eyebrows. She hadn't even thought about reporting it. But as much as she felt she should, part of Grace just wanted it to be over. She didn't want to poke the bear. Not anymore. 'Am I stupid if I say no?'

'You don't have to press charges, but it's not the worst idea to have it on record. Just in case.'

That was true. Besides, even though she'd stood up to him, Edward rarely gave up without a fight and she couldn't be certain he wouldn't hurt her again. 'Okay, we'll go. But first, tell me more about this threat.'

Luke told her what Edward had said, the insinuation and the look in his eyes. Grace's spine tingled.

'Cade reckons Edward's more talk than anything else, but Brett doesn't seem to agree. They'll go talk to him, which Mum and Dad are happy with. Dad said he'd watch Smithy's, but we've got cameras and an alarm system, so he's not too worried.'

Grace nodded, but her queasiness didn't ease. 'Dad's usually more talk than action, but anger has a way of making him lash out.'

He reached up to stroke her sore cheek. 'Like with this? Has he hit you before?'

'First time. But I think it wouldn't hurt for us to be careful over the next few days, though a visit from the police should be enough to deter him from doing anything drastic.' She hoped.

'All right. But, Grace ...' He smiled softly, his eyes glittering. 'No matter what your father threatened me with, it wouldn't have stopped me from being with you. I love you.'

Grace's heart swooned all over again. 'I love you. And thank you.'

His hands brushed up her arms. 'For what?'

'For giving me the Christmas I've always wanted. A happy one, with someone who cares about me.'

Smiling, Luke pulled her towards him and cupped her cheek. 'And I'll continue to do so, year after year. Because Grace ... you deserve to be cherished.'

Chapter Twenty-One

Nerves twisted in Grace's belly as she walked into the police station. Somehow, it felt wrong to make a statement against her father, but assault was assault, and she left half an hour later feeling stronger and proud of herself.

'You did well, Grace,' Luke said as they walked towards Smithy's where Grace's car remained parked.

'Thank you. I really hope we'll never have to use that statement, but you were right to put it on record.'

He pulled her close and placed a kiss in her hair. 'We'll be all right.'

Despite the niggling feeling in the back of her mind, for the first time, Grace actually believed that. 'We will.' She stepped away and smiled up at him. 'I'll be back at your place shortly.'

'Don't be long.'

She couldn't be as she climbed into her car. Now that the anxiety of spending Christmas with her family no longer lingered, excitement shimmied through her veins as she returned home, packed a bag, and rushed back to Luke's. They headed out for a sunset walk and made a warmed salmon and quinoa salad for dinner.

'Do you want to watch a Christmas movie?' Grace asked, pulling a few DVDs out of her bag. 'I have a couple, although they're mainly romcoms.'

'There's nothing wrong with romcoms,' he said, stirring the quinoa and glancing at the movies. 'You can put on *Love Actually.*'

Her eyebrows shot up. 'Really?'

'Sure. It's a good one and I haven't seen it since I was still living at home. Jessica used to watch it all the time, and you know how she hogs the TV. I always watched what she wanted.'

'Yeah, that sounds like Jess. Although I don't mind since we have similar tastes.'

She waited until dinner was ready, then set the movie to play as she curled up beside Luke to eat. When their dishes were empty, he turned off the lights and they snuggled beneath a blanket in the freezing air conditioning. Not that she was cold with his warm arms wrapped around her. This was all she could have asked for this Christmas, a relationship based on mutual support.

They went to bed after the movie singing, 'All I want for Christmas is you' and exchanged some gifts. Luke liked the jam and the soft bath towels she'd found at Elizadale Homewares. They were nothing special, but a useful item and in Cowboys colours, so she'd been happy with the find. She received new lavender soap and loved the Christmas themed patchwork throw blanket he'd chosen. Tossing it over them both, she huddled beneath the doona with Luke and woke on Christmas Day warm and content in his arms.

His lips found her neck and she grinned, curving her body into his and relishing in the merriment as they made love. But they couldn't lounge in bed all morning since they'd promised to meet his parents at the church service, so they showered, ate a quick breakfast, and strolled up the road to the Elizadale church.

Mary and Nick Smithfield welcomed her with open arms.

'Merry Christmas, Grace.' Mary hugged her and kissed her cheek. 'I'm so pleased to have you join us.'

'I hope I'm not imposing at such late notice.'

Mary dismissed the concern with a wave of her hand. 'No one can impose at Christmas. I'll admit, I was disappointed when Luke told me you wouldn't be joining us for any part of the day. It's been too long since he's dated a nice girl and I can't tell you how glad I am that he's found you.'

Grace's heart swelled just as a thin arm wrapped around her shoulders and Jessica slipped up beside her. 'Just let me remind you, she was *my* friend first.' Grinning, Jessica squeezed Grace tight. 'But I agree with Mum. You deserve to be happy, Grace, and we're going to have the best Christmas.'

Grace smiled softly, emotion bubbling inside her as she slipped into a pew between Jessica and Luke. He held her hand as she studied the program, not knowing what to expect as she'd never been to church, let alone on Christmas Day. But she thoroughly enjoyed herself as she listened to the Christmas Story and sang some of her favourite carols. Many of the regulars weren't there as she didn't see Meg, Sue, or Rebecca Taylor around, but everyone wished each other a merry Christmas, then Luke took her home where they could change out of their church wear and into something more suitable for backyard cricket. She pulled on her shorts and a cute red top, then Luke turned from the dresser with a small gift in his hand.

Grace froze. 'I thought we'd exchanged gifts last night.'

'Yes, but this one is the extra special present I wanted to save for today.'

Heat rose into her cheeks. 'Oh, Luke. No. I didn't get you anything special.'

'That's where you're wrong. And I loved my jam,' he added before Grace could question him. 'But I saw these in Cairns and thought they suited you.'

Grace reached out and accepted the gift. 'I guess I'm just not used to feeling special ...'

Chuckling, he reached to cup her chin and lift her gaze to his. 'Get used to it, Grace.' His lips swooped down to brush over hers.

Belly fluttering, she unwrapped the gift, her heart lurching at the sight of the jewellery box. Turning it in her hands, she flipped open the lid.

Her breath caught as the light flickered off the teardrop rubies dangling on diamond studs. 'Oh, Luke. They're beautiful.'

His arm came around her and drew her close. 'I thought you'd like them.'

Tearing her gaze from the earrings, she met his sparkling blue eyes and smiled. 'I do.' They were frivolous, unnecessary, and utterly meaningful. 'Best Christmas present ever.'

* * *

Luke watched Grace as she cracked a bonbon with his mother, squealing in joy as she won and dug out the paper hat.

She read the corny joke, everyone laughed, then she fitted the flimsy red hat around her head. If his heart swelled any further, his chest would burst.

She looked so right sitting in his parents' dining room, and not just because she'd been there many times before as Jessica's friend. She was his and he'd meant what he'd said yesterday when he'd confessed that he loved her. There was nothing Edward White could have told him that would deter his feelings for Grace. Luke hated what he'd done to her and the pain he'd caused. No one deserved that kind of emotional abuse, and the fact Edward had hit her made Luke's blood boil. It'd taken everything inside him not to storm out to White Peaks and lay into the bastard, but with Edward's threat lingering in the back of his mind, the police had agreed it would be best they kept their distance.

Besides, it was Christmas. Time to relax, be merry, and for him and Grace to revel in their love.

Though how he could love a woman who was hopeless at cricket was beyond him.

'All you have to do is hit the ball!' he called from the other side of the yard.

'It's not that easy!'

'Yeah, mate, cut her some slack,' his dad said. 'It's not like your mother can bowl.'

'It's only supposed to be fun,' his mum said, tossing the ball between her hands. 'You boys can get serious tomorrow.'

Elizadale's Boxing Day test was anything but serious, but at least the men who gathered the next day knew how to play cricket. They traditionally drew straws to split into teams, and Grace was there to cheer him on as they played a few overs until calling it at lunch.

Luke's team won.

But then the festivities came to a close and Luke poured himself into the preparations for the New Year. Jessica organised decorations, his father gave his final opinion on the cocktail menu, and his mother made last-minute changes to the bistro while Luke kept his attention on the kitchen. Nervous excitement continued to shimmy through him as they stocked the new herbs and spices, cut up dozens of pineapples for freezing, prepared mini vegetable spring rolls, and stashed bags of corn chips in the pantry. It might not be Luke's usual job, but he enjoyed working alongside Bill and the two kitchen staff and seeing his dreams unfold. They received their first delivery of avocados from Jade Farm, and Bill used the last bag of frozen chips on the evening of the twenty-ninth. Luke rarely stayed late on a Wednesday, but he wanted to be there when they served their last chicken parmies, crumbed steaks, and shut off the deep fryers for the last time.

'Well, that's it then, boss,' Bill said as he began wiping down the kitchen. 'I'll clean up a bit in here, then see you tomorrow to turn this place over.'

Luke nodded. They'd closed the kitchen tomorrow to allow them time to do a thorough clean and refit the new appliances before the thirty-first.

Then they'd launch Smithy's into the New Year.

* * *

Edward's hand tightened around the phone. 'What do you mean he's no longer available?'

'I've sold exclusive rights to Wally,' Matt Clark replied, clipped and businesslike. 'I had another cattleman approach me who's going into wagyu beef and with the herd he needs to cover and my own, Wally will be unavailable for any more servicing.'

'It's a fucking bull! Its sole purpose is to produce semen for service!'

'Yet even a bull can only safely produce so much, White. If I over-service him, it'll reduce his production quality and value.'

The fucking animal was headed for the meatworks, anyway. What did it matter if his use expired early? 'You promised me that bull, Clark.'

'I promised no such thing, White. It's business, and I had to do what was best.'

'You're doing this because Grace dumped you.'

Matt snorted. 'I have more pride than that, White. Your daughter might have been a loss, but she's not the only woman out there and I'm not one to grovel. If things had worked out between us, we might have become family and done some good deals, but unfortunately, it's not meant to be.'

'We'll see.' Having had enough of the kid's gloating, Edward slammed the receiver down. Fucking bastard, undermining him like that. How dare he sign away exclusive rights just to protect the bull's balls! You'd think the animal would get a thrill out of covering more heifers. Although he wouldn't cover them, rather have the vet jerk him off.

Gritting his teeth, Edward twisted the lid off the whiskey. This was all his daughter's fault. She'd upset her mother by not coming for Christmas and lost him the best chance he'd had in years to save the property. All for fucking Smithfield, who didn't recognise a threat when it slapped him in the face.

Stupid fool would pay for that. The health nut had stolen his daughter, cost him Wally, and had everyone talking about some fancy-pants new menu that would undoubtedly help the backstabbing Smithfields flourish.

Hands clenching, Edward pushed away from the desk. Bloody bastards, the lot of them. They'd get what they deserved.

Reaching into the cabinet, Edward grabbed his shotgun.

Chapter Twenty-Two

Luke loved New Year's Eve. As a publican, it was one of the busiest nights of the year and sure, he had plenty of crazy, horrible stories about drunk customers to share and not everyone loved working that night. But the sense of one door closing and the other opening had always given him hope for new possibilities. A fresh start. Another chance. And as this year came to an end, he knew without a shadow of a doubt that the coming twelve months would be some of the best of his life with Grace by his side and a fresh start for Smithy's.

He arrived at the pub midmorning, a spring in his step as he slipped through the side door and into the office. Yesterday had been hectic and gruelling as he'd helped scrub the kitchen and overseen the installation of the new appliances. He and Bill had rearranged the kitchen, the air fryers were in, and Luke had agreed to upgrade the grill in the coming months since the old one was nearing the end of its days. The menus sat unblemished on the tables, the laminate intact having never been used, and full staff were on shift for tonight.

Luke's heart raced with anticipation.

So did Jessica's, it seemed, as she bounced into the office.

'I'm here! Are you excited, bro? It's going to be a big day. Good thing you've been working out as we're going to need those muscles to shake the cocktails tonight.'

Luke grinned. 'It'll be a good night, Jess. Look at us, hey? My new menu and your cocktail night both creating a buzz.'

'We're going to have a fabulous night. Mum and Dad should have put us in charge years ago.'

Luke laughed. 'It'll be a party, I'll give you that.'

'I think we should have a cocktail night every month,' she said, slipping her handbag into a locker. 'Maybe even a theme night?'

'What? Like Hawaiian?'

'Maybe.' Shrugging, she followed him out to the bar. 'We're off to a good start this year, Luke, and the menu will certainly change things, but there's more we could do to bring people in. Trivia's always fun and you know I've always wanted to do a paint and sip. Or—' Jessica drew to a halt. 'Do you hear that?'

He frowned. 'I don't hear—' Then he did. A soft beeping. Luke's frown deepened. Where was—

'Shit!' Heart leaping into his throat, Luke ran through the door into the bistro. The beeping grew louder. With Jessica on his heels, he pushed through the swinging doors into the kitchen.

Luke froze.

Jessica screamed, her hands shooting to her mouth. They both stared at the scene in abject horror.

The place was a mess. The fridge door lay open, the alarm beeped, and food was everywhere. Red sauce stained the walls, guacamole and hummus dripped from the ceiling. Lettuce, shredded carrot, and vegetables scattered over the floor. Luke's fists curled as he moved through the kitchen. His heart pounded. He couldn't breathe. Not that he wanted to as the summer heat didn't help with the smell. Ants had already made themselves at home. Flies too. He reached the fridge door and his jaw clenched so hard he was afraid he'd break teeth.

Spring rolls squashed on the floor, clearly marked with boot imprints. Pumpkin patties mixed with the pastry and dirt. Hundreds of plastic boxes filled with a week's worth of prep were cracked, broken, and thrown about.

The open freezer door on the other side showed even more carnage.

'Oh, Luke ...' Jessica's voice cracked. 'This is ... I can't ... who would do this?'

Every muscle in Luke's body clenched, vibrating with rage as he pushed his fists into his pockets. He knew who.

'Call Cade.'

* * *

Grace's breath rasped from her throat as she ran into Smithy's, pushed open the kitchen door, and almost skidded on shards of lettuce. Her hands flew to her mouth as she cried out in shock.

Luke had said it was bad, but she hadn't imagined this. Sauce acted as new paint while vegetables carpeted the floor.

She shook her head, unable to believe it as Luke left his discussion with Brett and Cade and strolled towards her. Grace threw her arms around him and burst into tears.

'I'm so sorry! This is all my fault. I never thought—'

Luke's arms squeezed around her as she fought for breath. 'Do *not* blame yourself. This is not on you, Grace.'

'But ... But I ...' Blinking back tears, Grace peered past

him and pressed her lips together as she took stock of the carnage. Guilt fought with rage as her hands fisted around Luke's shirt. This wouldn't have happened if Luke hadn't been dating her. But what could she have done? Give in to her father's schemes? Sacrifice her heart? Give Matt another chance?

No way in hell.

Teeth clenching, Grace stamped her foot. 'Ooh, I could kill him!'

'I know.' Luke's eyes blazed as he brushed his hands up and down her arms. 'Everything's ruined, Grace. The spring rolls. The salads. Nothing's cold anymore.'

As quickly as her anger had taken hold, Grace crumpled again and buried her face against his chest. 'I'm sorry, Luke.'

She should have known better. Her father always had an ace up his sleeve. He always got his way. She would never escape him and he would never give up his need to control her. To hurt her. To hurt the people she loved.

Luke had worked so hard and because she loved him, her father had destroyed his dream. Cost him time, money, and would make him look a fool when they had no food to serve this evening.

And she'd thought she couldn't hate her father any more.

Luke's lips brushed the top of her head. 'It's okay, Grace. Stop saying you're sorry.'

Realising she'd been muttering it over and over, Grace drew out of his hold. She met Jessica's gaze and blinked back more tears. 'I can't help it. I feel terrible.'

'Don't,' Jessica said kindly. 'You're not to blame for your father's actions.'

Brett nodded. 'If they were his, although I don't doubt it.'

'He denied threatening you on Christmas Eve, Luke,' Cade

said. 'But we'll go have a chat to him again and review your CCTV footage.'

'How did this happen?' Grace asked.

'The cameras and alarm were shot out.'

'Dad does own guns. Legally.'

Cade nodded. 'I know. After that, the door was smashed in and then this.' He gestured around them, disgust twisting his handsome face.

Grace didn't blame him, although her father would never cease to amaze her. Breaking into Smithy's was one thing, but this? He could have smashed bottles of rum, vandalised the furnishings, or burned the whole place down. She wouldn't put any of that past him. But Edward had known what he was doing and had gone after what would hurt her the most. She'd helped with the menu and now the launch was ruined. It would take all afternoon just to clean the place up and, with the weekend and Monday being a public holiday, they wouldn't be able to restock for days. Not to mention the time it would take to prep and regroup.

Closing her eyes, Grace took a deep, calming breath. Would it ever end? Edward had tried to separate her from Luke. He'd hit her. Belittled her. Committed a criminal act against the man she loved.

But dammit, she would *not* let him defeat her.

She glanced at Cade. 'Have you taken evidence?'

'I've collected some items and taken photos.'

'So, we can clean up?'

'Grace, you don't—'

She turned to Luke, determination steeling her spine. 'We haven't got much time. Smithy's opens for dinner in eight hours and we will *not* have no food to serve.'

'But we *have* no food!' he cried, turning in a circle. 'It's on the walls and ceiling. The fridge is a mess and the freezer's been out of temperature range for who knows how long. We can't—'

He shoved his hand through his hair and shook his head. Her heart plummeted along with his shoulders. But she would fix this. She had to.

Grace placed her hand on his chest. 'We won't have a full menu, Luke, but we *will* serve something. You've worked too hard and I cannot let my father win. He won't beat me and he won't beat you. So, let's make a few phone calls, clean up, and see what we can salvage.'

Luke's blue eyes met hers, uncertainty lingering. But after a moment, the clouds cleared, his shoulders straightened, and he reached for his phone.

'I'll call Bill. Jess, get Mum and Dad on the phone, and Grace—'

'I'm on it,' she said, already dialling.

Chapter Twenty-Three

Within minutes, all staff had gathered at the Smithfield Hotel. Bill and Luke's parents arrived, shocked and horrified by the scene, but undeterred. Bill muttered oath after oath, devastation etching his face as he swept up spring rolls and cleaned out the fridge and freezer. The staff had come without question and everyone rolled up their sleeves, tossing food out by the bucket load while Luke joined Bill in the search for anything salvageable. They'd been spared a few bags of corn chips from the top shelf and a bag of walnuts, but he doubted they'd have time to cook and cool pumpkin or source rocket to serve the pumpkin and walnut salad.

'We're in luck!' Bill called, emerging from the fridge. 'The lasagne at the back of the freezer is still frozen, boss.'

Luke's stomach clenched. 'You sure?'

'Positive. Buried deep in the back, away from the door. I wouldn't serve the ice cream, but lasagne doesn't thaw quickly. We have thirty serves.'

At least that was something. Luke glanced at his mother, where she stood with a notebook. 'We can keep lasagne on the menu.'

Within an hour and a half of calling the reinforcements, the kitchen sparkled, the smell had vanished, and Grace strode in from the bistro with a spring in her step.

'Good news! Vicki can have fresh ciabatta baked and delivered by mid-afternoon and Jade Farm is sending someone in with a heap of avocados. I've spoken with the supermarket and they're boxing up everything that we need, so we can keep the ciabatta with guacamole, hummus, and cashew dip for tonight.'

The tension in Luke's neck eased a fraction. 'Excellent.'

Grace beamed as she continued. 'We'll have to forgo the spring rolls, but the supermarket has plenty of brown rice, coconut, chickpeas, and all the herbs and spices we need. Dried, that is.'

'That's all good and well,' Bill said, 'but the chicken and steaks are no good. And we won't be able to serve prawn twisters.'

Grace winced. 'Yeah, I can't save the prawn twisters, but as for the rest, I made some calls and—'

'I have steak!' The doors clattered open and Samantha Hudson strode into the kitchen with a freezer bag in each hand. 'Now, I don't stock rib or eye fillets, but I have a few kilos of sandwich steak that Grace said you could use for burgers.'

Speechless, Luke stared at the bags while his mother hugged Samantha, tears in her eyes.

'Thank you,' she said. 'That's too generous.'

'It's what friends do, Mary. I just can't believe someone would want to ruin you guys like this.' Samantha shook her head, disgust twisting her lips. 'I sure hope they catch whoever it was.'

'The police are handling that,' Luke said, 'but right now,

we just want to launch the menu the best we can, so thank you, Samantha.'

She smiled. 'Let me know if there's anything else you need. I hope you do well tonight and I promise I won't say a word.'

'We appreciate that,' Luke said. They couldn't keep the vandalism a secret forever, but he wouldn't launch the new menu beneath the dark cloud Edward White had tried to draw over them. He wanted tonight to be a success and for the locals to come for the food. He wanted them to enjoy the menu and to remember the delicious meals on offer, not to speculate about vandalism and sabotage.

That's only if they could complete the menu, but over the following hour, it seemed like they wouldn't need to make many alterations as more people arrived to help. Georgina from the Royal Hotel brought ice cream, rump steak, and chicken. The takeaway store spared some of their Spanish mackerel and Vicki delivered freshly baked bread. His mother insisted everyone send invoices and Jessica returned from the produce store loaded up with potatoes, carrots, and beans. Then Wendy Maguire arrived from High Ridge and effectively completed their menu with homegrown tomatoes, heaps of lettuce, more chicken, and a generous hunk of roast lamb.

'I heard you needed a "roast of the day",' she said, sliding the seasoned meat into the oven. 'And I hope you don't mind, but I'd already had it marinating in one of my special blends. Although it's not that special and I'm happy to share the recipe if it's a hit tonight.' She glanced at Bill. 'Only if you'd like.'

Luke swallowed a laugh as the older man blushed. Wendy Maguire was a magician with food and rarely shared her five-star chef trade secrets.

'I'm sure it will be a hit, so I can't say no,' Bill mumbled. 'Thank you, Wendy.'

'Anything to help,' she said easily, and even though she likely had lots to do to prepare for her own New Year's bash at High Ridge, Wendy stayed another hour to help Bill prep the salads and make a fresh batch of hummus.

Slouching against the bench, Luke could hardly believe it as the kitchen staff bustled around him. The Royal, roadhouse, and Wendy Maguire might have their own restaurants to run and plans for the evening, yet they'd come to his aid in true Elizadale spirit. Competition or not, holiday or not, it didn't matter. His mother presented him with a newly printed placeholder menu for the evening, and Luke's chest tightened. Yet despite the emotional toll the day had taken, he couldn't contain his grin. They almost had the full menu on offer, missing only the pumpkin burgers, spring rolls, herb-encrusted salmon, and two salads.

His mother flopped into a chair and Jessica declared she needed a cocktail, even though she never drank at work. Bill, however, bounced around the kitchen. He wiped down the benches and prepared for service with newfound energy, an enthusiasm that Luke shared as he wrapped his arms around Grace and squeezed her tight.

He'd never felt more lonesome or drear than when he'd stood in the carnage earlier that day. Sure, he'd have pulled himself together, but the fact they were launching the menu on time was all down to the sheer determination of this strong and beautiful woman.

'Thank you, Grace. What you did ... pulling this together ...' His chest swelled until he hurt. 'You are amazing.'

Her eyes sparkled as her fingers spread over his chest. 'It was a team effort, Luke. Everyone wanted to help and see you succeed.'

'And you wouldn't be defeated.'

'Never again,' she said as she rose onto her toes and kissed him.

* * *

Edward denied any involvement in the break-in and vandalism, which didn't surprise Grace. He wasn't the kind of man who wanted to be caught and Cade didn't have the resources to examine ballistics around the cameras, as that would involve investigators from Cairns. Finger printing would also take time, and with the holidays, they would have nothing to convict Edward for weeks.

But one of the hotel guests reported he'd heard what he thought were gunshots, before passing it off as firework rehearsal. Another had seen a vehicle matching her father's speeding away from the pub at about one o'clock in the morning and CCTV at the roadhouse and the entrance to Shadow Creek had both caught the ute on the highway shortly afterwards.

With that evidence, Brett and Cade had made the arrest.

'Edward didn't have a response to the footage,' Brett said, leaning against the bar while locals crowded around them with cocktails in their hands and party hats on their heads. 'He denied it, of course, but cameras don't lie and it'll be enough to hold the charges. He'll be seen in court in the next few weeks and he'll pay a fine, plus compensation.'

Grace caught herself between a grin and a wince as she mixed the ice in her Diet Coke. 'He won't be happy about that.'

'It's less than he deserves, but it's the best we can do.' Brett straightened. 'I'm glad it worked out for you, though,

Smithfield. The menu looks delicious and I'll bring Linda in for dinner later in the week.'

'Thanks, Brett.' Luke extended his hand over the bar. 'Happy New Year to you.'

The sergeant left and Luke let out a deep breath, his forearms flexing as he leaned over the bar. Grace grinned as she unashamedly checked him out. Only four weeks had passed since she'd sat in this same spot gushing over the vegetarian lasagne and trying not to flirt with Luke, yet so much had changed. She'd overcome her fear and had stood up to her father against all odds. Christmas had been a delightful day that she'd celebrated with people who cared about her and who she loved in return. Her yoga classes would begin next week with a dozen people already booked in. And she'd found a man who would believe in her no matter what, one she could give her whole heart to and trust with every fibre of her being.

Nothing had stopped her from ensuring the menu launch tonight, and together, they relished their success. Bill had sold out of the lasagne; the coconut chicken on pineapple rice proved to be a popular order, and there had been no complaints about the lack of fries.

Except from good old Ben at the other end of the bar as he'd dug into his baked potato and seasoned chicken breast.

Bill shut down the kitchen at ten o'clock with Grace, Luke, and his parents there to pop open a bottle of champagne. Elated, Grace even had a celebratory sip, cringing at the burning taste.

'You were right, boss!' Bill cried, toasting Luke with his glass. 'This was a damn good idea. The locals loved the food.'

Grace smiled, leaning into Luke's solid body as his arm tightened around her.

'I never doubted it,' he said. 'But I couldn't have done it without my taste-tester here.' He pressed his lips to her hairline. 'I love you, Grace. Thank you for your support.'

Everything inside her melted. Support. That's all anyone needed. Support and encouragement from the people they loved. And for the first time in her life, Grace had that person to lean on.

Christmas truly was the time for miracles. 'I love you too.'

The evening ended on a high as she stood in Luke's arms behind the bar and counted down the seconds to midnight. Cheers, whistles, and party poppers erupted around them, and with hope in her heart, Grace kissed her man at the beginning of what would be a magnificent year.

Acknowledgements

The gratitude never ceases in writing and publishing as I could never produce my books without the fantastic team behind me. As always, thank you to the writing communities of Romance Writers of Australia and the Australian Romance Readers Association for your support. I am grateful for the opportunities and encouragement that you bring to your members, readers, and writers of romantic stories.

A heartfelt thank you goes to my wonderful editor Nicola for your thoughtful suggestions and for pointing out that perhaps I hadn't actually finished *The Pub with No Food*. Your editorial insight is invaluable, and I love working with you. Just as I love working with my amazing cover designer Danielle. Thank you for your epic cover and for bringing Grace and Smithy's to life. You always seem to know exactly what I need when I can't articulate it myself.

Thank you to my writing buddies Deeanna West, Barbara Strickland, and Jill Staunton. I cherish having you in my corner and thank you deeply for your beta-reading and feedback. Dee, sorry (not sorry) for how sexy this book is, and I'm so glad to have you in my corner. Barbara, I always welcome your encouragement and support. Jill, this was the first book we worked on together and I've valued your guidance ever since.

If we hadn't been inspired to write Christmas novellas, this story may never have been told, so what a treat that it's finally out there.

Thank you to Mum and Ian for your continued support in my writing career. It has been a wonderful journey so far with you cheering me on and acting as my market-stall 'roadies'. I honestly could not do this without you.

And of course, a heartfelt thanks to you, my dear reader. Whether you're continuing this journey with me or picking up one of my books for the first time, I'm honoured you chose to spend your time with my words. I hope you enjoyed and can welcome you back in Elizadale really soon!

The *Shadow Creek* series